MW00639595

THE INVISIBLE HOUSE

C.W. TASK

First Printing, September 2020
Copyright © 2020 by C.W. Task
All rights reserved.
ISBN-13: 978-0-9859976-8-7

Printed in the United States of America

This is a work of fiction. Names, characters, places, and incidents are either the products of the author's imagination or are used fictitiously. Any resemblance to actual events, locales, organizations, or persons, living or dead, is entirely coincidental.

The publisher does not have any control over and does not assume any responsibility for author or third-party web sites or their content.

The scanning, uploading, and distribution of this book via the Internet or via any other means without the permission of the publisher is illegal and punishable by law. Please purchase only authorized electronic editions, and do not participate in or encourage electronic piracy of copyrighted materials. Your support of the author's rights is appreciated.

FICTIONSMITH

fictionsmith.com

The text type was set in Adobe Caslon Pro

For everyone who felt a little lost
when they suddenly found
time on their hands.

The Invisible House

ONE

EIGHT AND A HALF HOURS WAS ABOUT AS LONG AS Oliver and I could travel at a time.

Of course, the trip was easier for Oliver because he was our family's van, but the funny sounds he had been making matched how my stomach felt after such a long family drive.

Dad turned up the radio to try and ignore the squeaking sound coming from the engine. Mom just kept flipping through her book even though she always said it made her carsick to read on the road.

Next to me, my little sister, Daisy, who we called Petals for short...even though Petals has six letters and Daisy only has five...had fallen asleep again in her carseat. She was drooling a little, and Dad's music almost covered up her snoring.

I saw her crayons and coloring book had dropped to the van's floor, so I reached down and put them on her lap so she would be surprised when she woke up.

"Almost there!" Dad called out.

I celebrated with a thumbs up, then turned my head to see our new neighborhood. Really, I wasn't very excited about moving away from my friends and school, but there was something thrilling about coming to a new state.

Mom had kept going on about how much she loved something called mid-century modern style houses, and a lot of the buildings seemed like they could have come out of a science-fiction book.

It was time to play my favorite math game where I would read the sides of the mailboxes and try to add up the numbers together as quickly as I could. Five plus three plus eight was sixteen…five plus three plus four was twelve…even though it was summer, I was afraid I would fall behind in my new school once I started fifth grade in the fall.

I saw two kids about my age riding on their bikes going the other direction. I would have to meet them after we got our bags moved into the new house.

"Mom?" I asked, "Can I take my bike around the neighborhood to make some friends?"

"Maybe after we get a little more familiar with the place," Mom said. "We don't want you getting lost."

"I wouldn't be lost if I made friends who knew their way around," I said, giving my most innocent smile.

"It's family movie night!" Dad said, turning the van down another street. "We can't miss our favorite family tradition!"

As Oliver turned and gave a squeal of protest, I saw why the van was complaining. Ahead, the road rose into a super steep hill.

"Do we live up there?" I asked, eyes wide.

"Sure do!" Dad said proudly. "We'll be able to see the whole neighborhood."

As we reached the top of the hill, we pulled into the driveway of a brown brick two-story house that was way older than the one we had just moved from. Mom made the sound she usually does when she is surprised, but not in a good way. "Well, I've always liked painted brick," she said. "Maybe a nice cream color would do."

"That's the spirit," Dad said.

Coming to a stop, Oliver made a loud bang, which woke up Petals.

"I'm awake!" she shouted. "Dibs on my own room!"

"We're not getting our own rooms, Petals," I said.

"I'm not Petals, I'm a sea dragon," my sister said, rubbing her eyes. She always seemed to want to pretend she was something else and I had a hard time keeping up with her four-year-old imagination.

"Okay, sea dragon–"

"But I can turn into a hedgehog when I want to." She held up the sheet of paper in her lap. "Like this."

Squinting at the artwork, I was glad she had told me what it was. "Wait," I said, "how many bedrooms are there?"

"Four," Mom replied. "One for me and Dad, one for you two girls, a guest room, and the nursery for when baby boy arrives." She unbuckled herself and climbed out of the car, giving a big stretch.

'Baby boy' was going to change a lot of things. He wasn't even here yet and he was already getting his own room.

I went to the back of the van and patted Oliver, hoping he would feel better soon. Dirt came off on my hand, showing the real olive color beneath the mess from the road. I wiped the dirt on my pant leg, getting a raised eyebrow from Dad.

I pulled out my duffel and sleeping bag and then helped Petals find her favorite stuffed bear she called Teddo. She had somehow thrown him into the back of the van during the drive through Kentucky.

I tried to imagine what the hill must have been like before our place was built. There wasn't much of a front yard, and the hill didn't have enough space for more than two houses that shared a circular driveway.

As I walked through the brown front door, the dusty house smell tickled my nose, but Dad said it was just the scent of potential. I thought it smelled like Mom was going to ask us to mop and dust right away.

4

"Which room is ours?" I asked, holding up my sleeping bag.

Dad shook his head, and tossed his own bag in the middle of the empty living room. It left a clean streak where dust used to be when it landed on the wood floor. "Family camp out, my dear. Without our furniture, we might as well all sleep in here." He smiled. "Going to be a big night, so we are–"

"Ordering Chinese food?" I asked hopefully.

Dad put a finger on his nose. I had guessed right.

Mom held up her phone. "I'll put in the order."

"Can I get my bike and check out the neighborhood?" I asked. "I promise I'll be back before the food arrives."

Dad checked his watch, then glanced over to Mom. "It's not like we have any more unpacking to do," he said.

Mom shrugged, focused on the menu.

"Okay, knock yourself out," Dad said. "But don't really knock yourself out."

"We should probably check where the nearest hospital is, just in case," Mom said.

With a little bit of help from Dad, I got my bike off of the back of Oliver. My eyes went wide when I saw the big hill stretch out down below, then I felt a tap on my shoulder.

"Might want to take these," Dad said, offering my helmet and a walkie-talkie. He pressed the button

5

on the side and his voice came out sounding funny on my end. "Home Base to Chuckles. Come in, Chuckles, do you read me?"

"You can say Charlotte."

"We all need call signs," Dad protested. "That way we can't have our identities intercepted by the enemy."

I raised my eyebrow, then held the walkie-talkie up to my lips. "10-4, Home Base. Just let me know when Operation Chopsticks is a go." I tapped the walkie-talkie. "You know, it would be easier if I had a phone. We could even keep using the nicknames."

"That's a big time negative, Chuckles," Dad said. "Points for the sense of humor though." He winked. "Over."

"Be back soon," I said, putting the walkie-talkie in my purple bike's handlebar basket.

"Hey, hold up," Dad said, getting down on one knee. When he did that I knew he wanted to tell me something important. I walked my bike back over to him.

"What's up?"

Dad looked off at the neighborhood, then back at me. "Just wanted to tell you that I'm proud of how you're handling this move," he said. "I know it's not easy."

I nodded. I already missed my friends a lot. They were all ten hours away now.

"But we're going to have a lot of adventures here," Dad said. "Just remember who you are out there."

We had talked through this so many times before. "I know, Dad," I said. "I'm a Jones, and I'll act like one."

"Which means?"

"Be kind, help others…and…"

"Always carry a walkie-talkie."

I laughed. The third part of our family motto was never the same, which kept me on my toes.

"And watch for cars," Dad said, tapping me on my helmet.

"We have four things now?" I asked, buckling the strap.

"It's just good advice," Dad said, then turned to head back toward the house. "Have fun!"

I took off, carefully making my way down the steep hill.

It was going to be a pain to walk the bike back up.

As I gained speed, the walkie-talkie shifted in my basket and I tried to catch it. But moving to grab it took me off-balance and I lost the grip on my pedals. Before I could get control back, I was starting to fly down the hill.

Ahead, I came to a traffic circle and had to swerve to miss a mail truck. The mailman yelled something as I flew by and I shouted back an apology when I finally got control over my brakes.

7

Scanning the mailboxes, I traced my way back to the entrance of the neighborhood. I have a pretty good memory, so I found where we first drove through because of the math trick I had done when Oliver entered the neighborhood.

I began to take in the place. If I was going to live here for a while, I wanted to know it inside and out. I took in the smell of freshly cut grass and the tinkle of wind chimes in the air as the warm summer breeze pushed against my face. In the neighborhood park, two dogs barked at each other as their owners played tug of war with their leashes and said they were sorry over and over.

Then something buzzed in from above. It almost sounded like an airplane, but way closer than it should have been.

I tilted my head back, trying to spot where the sound was coming from, and was surprised to see a small, one-manned flying machine with a big fan on the back and a parachute above it.

The pilot waved down at me. I tried to return the wave, but lost control of my handlebars as my trusty bike decided to stop riding on the sidewalk and into some dirt.

My front tire hit something and I was flung over my handlebars and onto my back. With the wind knocked out of me, I tried to suck in some air as I watched the flying machine circle around me like a buzzard.

I sat up and saw what my bike had hit. A section of the sidewalk was completely missing, but I hadn't noticed because of the flying man. My tire had clipped a mailbox, but there was something odd about it.

There was no house behind the mailbox.

Two

Ow.

I sat up, checking myself for any cuts, and found a tear in my jeans around my left knee. I'd need to ask Mom to fix that, but I only had one more change of clothes until the movers came with our stuff, so I was stuck with these pants for now.

Seeing the grassy lot behind the mailbox, I started to wonder why there wasn't a house there. What was the point?

The mailbox had fresh black paint and brass around the edges, so it didn't seem abandoned or anything, but it wasn't like the other mailboxes on the street.

I checked to see if there was a name written on the side. *Nope.* It was blank but had some shiny numbers that said 924.

I knew it was illegal to open someone else's mail, but I wasn't sure what the rule was on just opening the mailbox and taking a teeny, tiny peek.

As my hand reached the latch, I heard a car approach and someone yelled, "Hey! That isn't yours, young miss."

My hand flew back and I turned to see the mailman I had almost run into when I flew down the hill. "Sorry."

The boxy mail truck pulled up next to me and an older, white haired man with a bushy mustache leaned out. He seemed more amused than mad as he stopped the car.

"Two-Seventeen Carefree Valley, eh?" he asked.

"Sorry, what?"

"You're new," he said, leaning on the steering wheel. "I guess it makes sense you wouldn't know your address yet."

"Carefree Valley?" I asked. "But we live on a big hill."

The mailman chuckled. "Oh, we get a laugh out of that one. Must have been a joke for the neighborhood developers. My name is Otto, by the way."

I didn't know if I should tell him my name since he was both a stranger and had yelled at me, but I figured it would be better to be kind, and I would probably see him a lot in the future. "Charlotte Jones."

"Oh," he said, raising his eyebrows like he knew my name already. "Nice to meet you, Miss Carefree Valley Charlotte." He glanced both ways as though

11

he was about to share a secret. "Sorry I yelled, but rules are rules, even when they are about one of the neighborhood mysteries."

My eyes widened. "*One* of the mysteries? What else goes on here?" Suddenly the idea of living in a new place got me a lot more excited.

"You've barely gotten settled in, so I'm sure you'll have all summer to discover them." Otto shifted his car out of park and was about to drive away.

"Wait," I said. "Can you at least tell me about the mailbox?"

Otto scrunched his nose and his mustache twitched from side to side. He pointed at the empty lot. "Hmm, well, some kids call that the invisible house."

"What do you call it?"

"I call it 'Forward to P.O. Box'…well, I can't say where. That's private. But, if you want to snoop around the neighborhood, check out the gnome houses," he said, pointing toward the forest across the street. "They're all over the place. But I'm running late. I'm sure I'll see you around, Miss Carefree Valley Charlotte."

He drove the truck down the street, ignoring the rest of the mailboxes. *Had he already delivered mail to those?*

The forest across the street had a trail leading into it, and I knew if I headed down there I would wind up getting lost without mailboxes to track my way home. And I didn't want to miss Operation Chopsticks.

Then I heard something that sounded like baseball cards in spokes down the street. Picking up my bike, I clipped the walkie-talkie onto the basket and made sure it wasn't broken. I put the chain back on the gear and wiped the grease from my fingers off on my pant leg next to the rip.

I took off toward the sound and before too long I found the two kids I had seen when we drove into the neighborhood.

They had ditched their bikes at a little park and were checking out some kind of giant birdhouse.

"Hi," I said, waving as I got close. I'd never really had much of a problem meeting new people. Dad used to say when I was little I would run onto a playground full of kids I didn't know and shout, 'Hey! It's me, your friend, Charlotte Jones!'

The boy with short, blond hair looked up at me from a book and cocked his head. "Uh, hi?"

The dark haired girl with blue eyes and a yellow sundress smiled, then used the book she was holding to swat the boy. "Victor, where are your manners?" She turned to offer her hand to shake. "I'm Lila, and that's Victor. You new here?"

I nodded. "Just got in today."

"What grade you in?" Victor asked, paying more attention to his book than me.

13

"Going to be in fifth."

"Us too!" Lila said excitedly, clutching her book to her chest. "Oh, I do hope we get Ms. Moriah. She's the best. We're trying to get through our summer reading program." She pointed to the large birdhouse.

I noticed it was full of books instead of birds.

"What is this?" I asked.

"It's our little lending library," Lila said proudly. "People put books in here when they are finished with them, and Victor and I come and check pretty often to see what's new."

"Yeah, it doesn't count toward getting a pizza if you keep reading the same book over and over," Victor said. "Which is totally not fair."

Lila rolled her eyes. "Most of the time all we see are books our moms would read or ones on how to get rich quick."

Victor snorted. "Those things don't work. I tried to read one, but I got stuck on stuff about market index and diversification."

"At least you remembered the words," I offered. "That's good for vocabulary, right?"

"Doesn't get me rich if I don't know what they mean," Victor said, then nodded to his bike. "All I want is to buy more cards for my spokes."

I decided it was time to change the subject. "So, what's the deal with the invisible house?" I asked, pointing my thumb over my shoulder.

They both shrugged, looking at me like I was crazy.

"What about that flying machine–"

"You already saw Mr. Adams?" Lila asked. "Isn't it so cool? He's been flying around here for decades."

"He keeps telling me he won't take me for a ride," Victor said.

"I don't think he can fit a second person," Lila said.

All of a sudden, my walkie-talkie screeched. "Home Base to Chuckles. Do you read me, Chuckles? Over."

I felt my face going red. The nickname came from the time Dad made me laugh so hard milk squirted out of my nose. It was fine for him to call me that, but it wasn't something I wanted other people to know. I hurried to grab the walkie-talkie. "Uh, hey Dad."

"That's not my call sign, Chuckles. Over."

I held down the walkie-talkie. "Sorry, it's my dad."

"Chuckles?" Victor asked.

I didn't feel like explaining the nickname, so I pressed the button to talk. "Home Base, I'm talking with some new friends. Can we pause the call sign?"

"Oh, perfect!" Dad said. "You should invite them to your birthday party on Friday."

Victor and Lila seemed embarrassed for me.

"Can we talk about this later?"

"Roger that. Operation Chopsticks is a go," Dad said. "Home Base over and out."

15

"Birthday party?" Victor asked. "Like with cake?"

Lila shot him a glare. "That's not why you go to someone's birthday party."

"It kind of is," he said with a shrug.

"Maybe we can talk to our parents," Lila said.

"No pressure or anything," I said, then pointed back toward the hill where my house was. "Dinner's ready. Got to go. Nice meeting you." I picked up my bike and headed off quickly before they could say anything.

Walking my bike up the hill was as tough as I thought it would be, and I felt gross and sweaty by the time I made it inside.

At least the ceiling fan was running because Mom likes it cold in the house.

The Chinese food was set out on our wobbly, green card table and Petals kept trying to dig in even with Mom getting on to her. Dad had to pick her up and put her on his shoulders to keep her away from the fortune cookies.

I stepped over the sleeping bags and pillows on the living room floor all ready for the family camp-in.

"How was the recon mission?" Dad asked, which I could barely hear over Petals squealing that he was going to run her into the ceiling fan.

"Okay," I said. "I found out there are gnome houses in–"

"What happened to your pants?" Mom cried.

"Gnome houses?" Dad asked.

16

"I'm a hedgehog!" Petals squealed, swinging her arms and legs without any effect on Dad.

"I wrecked my bike, but I'm okay," I said. "Sorry."

"I used to search for those in the woods when I was your age," Dad said, putting Petals down, who curled into a ball. "People store secret messages in them. Maybe we can go and see what's out there tomorrow morning before I start work."

Suddenly, our new house started to rumble, and one of the Chinese food cartons fell off of the card table.

THREE

I STEPPED OVER THE SPILLED FRIED RICE AND
followed Mom and Dad out the front door to see
what was causing all the shaking. The rumble grew
so loud, I couldn't think straight.

"What on Earth?" Mom cried, throwing her arms
in the air. "How is this okay?"

I bumped into her on the front porch and saw the
flying machine had landed and was circling in the
driveway between the two houses.

With a flick of a switch, the engine died, letting
me have my thoughts back. When I had seen this
thing flying in the sky on my adventure, I didn't
expect it to land right next to us.

"Don't worry," Dad said, giving Mom a pat on the
shoulder. "I'll handle this." He approached the pilot
and shouted, "Wow, that looks like fun!"

Mom wasn't pleased. "My turn," she said. When
Mom took her turns I always wanted to see what

happened, but also kind of wanted to hide until it was all over.

The pilot stepped out of his machine, put his flight goggles on top of his helmet, then took out his ear plugs. With a friendly wave, he smiled at us. Then he saw Mom approaching.

Our neighbor took his helmet off, showing a wild mess of white hair that he had to brush out of his eyes. He reminded me of a shaggy old sheep dog who liked to fly.

"Who are you?" Mom demanded, stopping just in front of him.

"First off, my name is Xavier Adams, and this here is *Betsy*," he said, patting the flying machine with a yellow and green paint job. "Well, *Betsy the Seventh*. And secondly, I have been given a grandfathered permit to fly from the homeowner's association since *Betsy the Second*."

That slowed Mom down a bit. "Well…it's nice to meet you, Xavier," she said. She wrapped her hands around her very pregnant belly. "I'm going to have to warm up to *Betsy*."

"Oh, don't you worry about me messing with the little one's nap times," Mr. Adams said. "As long as they don't try to sleep around 8 a.m. and 5 p.m. every other day. If the old girl doesn't get her regular exercise, she starts to fall apart fast. Learned that the hard way with *Betsy the Third*."

"Funny how the people who sold us this house didn't mention anything about you…or *Betsy*," Mom said.

Mr. Adams had started to fold up the parachute on the street. "Can't imagine why."

Petals ran with her arms out, making her best airplane noises with her mouth and going in circles until she got dizzy and fell down. Mom helped my sister up to her feet, then headed back inside as Petals returned to flight.

"See? The little one gets it," Mr. Adams said. He then locked eyes with me for a few seconds and cocked his head to the side. "Oh, it's you."

I lifted my eyebrows. "Huh?"

He shook his head and chuckled. "Sorry, I mean you're the one who wrecked their bike by that mailbox, right? Did you break anything?"

I blushed at the question. "No," I said. "I'm okay." Then an idea hit me. Mr. Adams had been flying above these houses for years and years. Maybe he knew something about the mailbox. "So, you know about the invisible house?"

"Oh, sure," he said. "Everybody likes to check it out around here."

Dad laughed. "What are you two talking about?"

Mr. Adams finished packing up the parachute and began walking *Betsy* into his garage. "C'mere, it's easier to just show you."

Dad nodded that it was okay to follow, and together we crossed the street and into Mr. Adams's garage.

Inside, the walls were covered with big photos of the neighborhood through the years. The earliest ones were black and white and showed a few houses down a main street, and Mr. Adams's house was all alone at the top of the hill. The rest of the picture was just forest.

The next one over had more houses and less forest. A few photos down, the pictures started showing up in color.

"There," Mr. Adams said, pointing to a house with some rectangles on top of its roof. "See that one?"

"Oh, yeah," Dad said, tapping the house on the picture. "The one with the solar panels?"

"Yep," Mr. Adams said. Then he walked deeper into the garage, tapping each picture where the house was until he reached a photo that said 1983 at the bottom. "Here."

His finger covered up the house. "What's special about that one?" I asked.

Mr. Adams lifted his finger, showing the house was gone. It was nothing but an empty lot and mailbox. "One day, the house was there, the next..." He puffed out his cheeks and opened his hands wide. "Poof. Gone."

"Was there a fire?" I asked.

21

"Not that I remember," Mr. Adams said. "It's one of the mysteries of the neighborhood."

"Do you remember who lived there?" I asked.

"Doctor...something," Mr. Adams said, putting his hand to his chin. "Dr. Rick? No. Fred? Maybe it was Dr. Fred Rick."

I felt Dad put a hand on my shoulder. "We should probably get the hedgehog out of the middle of the street."

"I'm a mermaid hedgehog!" Petals said.

"That can fly?" I asked.

Petals stopped and gave me a serious look as though I had asked a very silly question. "When I want to."

"Oh, don't worry about it," Mr. Adams said with a wide smile. "Nobody drives up here except me, the mailman, and now you all."

"Thank you for the help," I said.

At least now I had a name for who owned the mailbox, and the mystery continued.

Four

WE SAID GOODBYE AND WALKED BACK TO HAVE OUR dinner. The sweet and sour chicken flavored with floor dust could have tasted a little bit better, but at least this time I almost had chopsticks mastered.

Next up, we had family movie night, which was a game Dad had come up with when I was six years old as a way to get me using my imagination more.

Dad wrote some names of famous characters on scraps of paper and we each had to pick one to act out like we were somehow all in the same story.

Mom picked first and got Anne of Green Gables. She would never show us what she had, so sometimes I wondered if she just told us what she wanted to be. Dad wound up as the detective Sherlock Holmes. I was a little jealous because I had started to feel like a detective myself with the case of the invisible house.

Petals picked Tinker Bell.

Actually, she got someone named Rasputin, but since she couldn't read, she wound up as Tinker Bell because she loves fairies.

Lastly, I picked Dorothy from the Wizard of Oz. I remembered watching the movie for the first time and wondering why everything looked brown until she wound up in Oz and then the world became so full of color.

Dad got his phone out and we ran to the backyard. He propped it up on some patio bricks facing the woods behind our house and we all got to a place where the phone could see us.

The story wound up being about Sherlock Dad trying to figure out who had stolen the last fortune cookie.

It was an open and shut case once he saw Petals had the piece of paper with her lucky numbers and fortune sticking out of her mouth. There was an exciting chase scene when Tinker Bell jumped into an old tire swing in our backyard and pretended to fly away.

Afterward, we headed back inside to have our family 'camp in,' and it took me a long time before I felt comfortable in my sleeping bag on the floor.

I drifted off to the sounds of the new place creaking and settling as I wondered what an invisible house would look like if I could see it.

Before I knew it, the rumble from Mr. Adams's flying machine starting up across the street woke me up. As my eyes shot open, I noticed sunlight was already creeping in through the windows.

"It's six-thirty in the morning!" Mom yelled, checking her watch. "What is he thinking?"

"I'll talk to him," Dad said, slowly rolling out of his sleeping bag. He leaned over and shook my leg. "Hey kiddo. Maybe if we get up early enough, we'll see some gnomes still sleeping in their houses."

I got changed into the only other outfit from my duffel bag, picking out my favorite purple and pink shirt, and joined Dad out on the front porch.

Mr. Adams waved at us and shouted, "Sorry about that! Just a quarterly maintenance day. Won't happen again for three months."

"I'll mark my calendar," Dad said, waving back. "Maybe that could happen later in the day? We'll have another little one by then."

We got a thumbs up from Mr. Adams as he ducked back into his garage.

The air felt so nice, and the houses and forest down below were covered in a beautiful mist that made the whole place seem like it was from a fairy tale.

"Pretty amazing, isn't it?" Dad said.

"It's like I could find a unicorn in those woods if I got up early enough," I said.

Dad turned to me. "Well, we'd have to build a fence for the yard if you did," he said, stretching his back. "Let's give Mom and Petals a little more sleep and see if we can't find one of those gnome houses. Besides, I don't have any work calls until later this morning anyway."

Since Otto hadn't really mentioned exactly where the gnome houses were besides being in the forest, I took Dad down the hill toward where I had found the mailbox. Once we had made it into the fog, everything sounded weird and I had to rub my arms to try and keep warm.

"Pretty mysterious," Dad said, scanning the empty lot. The strange thing was that the place beyond the mailbox where the house should have been didn't have any fog in it.

What if the house was still there, but it really was invisible? I wondered as I searched for a small rock to toss and test my idea, but Dad grabbed my arm.

"Look," Dad whispered. "A fox." He pointed at the small red animal as it spied us from across the street, then darted into the woods down the trail.

"That's where the mailman said the gnome houses were," I said.

Dad nodded. "Okay, we should be careful then," he said as he led me across the street, looking both ways.

"So, what are we searching for?" I asked as I tried to see where the trail began in the fog. "What does a gnome house even look like?"

"Every one is different," Dad said. "Sometimes they are made up like mushrooms. Sometimes they are just little doors covering up a big knot in a hollow tree. It really depends on what the person who made it wanted to do with it."

A small part of me felt dumb for hoping that gnomes were really the ones who built them. I would have believed something like that when I was Petals's age.

Out of the corner of my eye, I saw something move and realized it was just a small creek with bubbling water. I began to walk toward it when Dad stopped me.

"Hey!" Dad said, inching closer to something I couldn't see yet. "Found one." He pointed to a low branch on a large tree a little bit down the walking path.

I followed where he pointed and saw a fake red and white mushroom, bigger than I had ever seen before. Next to it stood a jolly gnome statue, leaning with one hand on the mushroom.

"Go ahead," Dad said. "Look closer."

I walked slowly to the mushroom and saw it had a small brown door at the base with a little knob. Pulling it open ever so gently, I peeked inside to find...*nothing*.

"Well, that's no fun," I said, turning back to Dad. "I thought you said these things had secret messages."

"Maybe there's a trick to it," Dad said.

The gnome stared off into the distance with his goofy grin. "What are you so happy about?" I asked. While the gnome used one of his hands to lean on the mushroom house, the other hand reached up to his hat.

There was a little bit of a gap between his hand and his cone hat. He seemed more like a cookie jar than a statue.

Reaching over, I grabbed the hat and lifted. It easily came off. Inside the top of the hat was a small hole with a rolled up piece of paper. My eyes went wide and I dumped out the message into my hand.

Unrolling it, I saw some neat writing, small like a tooth fairy note.

It said:

> *To the person who found this,*
> *all I can say is, thank you from the*
> *bottom of my heart.*
> *–Susanna Friedrich*

FIVE

"SUSANNA FRIEDRICH," I SAID, TURNING THE PAPER over to see if anything was written on the back. It was blank. "Like Dr. Fred?"

"Or Dr. Rick," Dad said. "Maybe Mr. Adams meant Fred...Rick. Friedrich."

"I wonder if Susanna is his daughter," I said, tracing my finger over the swooping, cursive letters. The paper was yellow but it had probably started out white like the kind I use. In the top right corner I could see the handwritten date of August 1, 1968. I did the math in my head on how long ago that was. It was at least before Dad and Mom were born.

Dad leaned over my shoulder so he could read it too. "I think they wrote it with a fountain pen." He took the note and held it up to the sky. "No invisible ink or anything." He shrugged. "Well, someone wanted to show you some thanks."

"I wonder if she still lives in this neighborhood."

"Doubt it," Dad said, slowly checking out the forest. "Most people don't live in the same neighborhood they grew up in."

Down the trail I could still see the mailbox. What if she had lived in the house with Dr. Friedrich before it disappeared?

"Well, even with all of this excitement, I could use some coffee," Dad said, rubbing his eyes. "One gnome house down...who knows how many left to find?"

Part of me really wanted to stay and do some more searching in case there was another secret message from Susanna.

I started to wonder why she wanted to thank anyone who found her message...and why it had taken so many years for someone to find it.

I held onto the note since I guessed it was supposed to be for me. The fog had started to lift and the woods didn't feel mysterious anymore.

"Do you think Susanna was lonely?" I asked as we followed the trail to the other side of the small forest. It let out by the little park with the lending library.

"What makes you ask that?" Dad asked.

I shrugged. "She left a note for someone else and nobody found it while she was still a kid."

"Well, if she wanted to connect with someone, she probably shouldn't have hidden a message in a gnome hat," Dad said, peeking inside the lending library. "Or, maybe she hoped someday she would meet someone who had a curious mind like yours and it took longer than she thought it would."

"So you're going to search for her?" I asked, hopeful.

Dad nodded. "I'll see what I can find out about her and that mailbox."

As we started the walk up the hill to our house, I leaned in and gave my dad a hug. He patted me on the back, then picked me up and carried me like a football. I kicked and laughed until he had to put me down. He was breathing hard. "When did you get so big, kiddo?"

When we opened the front door, I could hear Mom in the kitchen.

"Oh, good, you're back," she said as she washed her hands in the kitchen sink. "The breakfast menu is set. You can either have toast with peach jam, or peach jam with toast. And the toast is more like bread unless you want to put it in the oven." She leaned against the counter. "I'm really ready for the moving truck to get here." She clapped her hands. "Petals! Breakfast is ready."

Petals was still completely in her sleeping bag. Breakfast was more ready for her than she was for it. "I'm not Petals, I'm—"

31

"A mermaid hedgehog?" Dad asked.

"No." Her voice was muffled by the bag. "I'm a caterpillar in a cocoon."

"Must be a growth spurt," Dad said as he used his pocket knife to slap a glob of peach jam onto some bread. With breakfast in his mouth, he went over and grabbed his laptop at the other end of the kitchen island.

"We saw a fox," I said to Mom, who thought most four legged animals who lived in forests were cute.

"Did he have a gnome riding on his back?" she asked.

"Funny you should say that," I said.

"Aha!" Dad cried, typing on his computer louder than he needed to. "Found something."

I rushed over to peek around him and read the title of the website. "Tax records?"

"Sherlock Dad is on the case," he said. "924 Duffy Lane is owned by a Dieter Friedrich, who has been paying his property tax since 1956. Already paid up for this year too…"

"Does he own another house somewhere?" I asked.

Dad narrowed his eyes at the screen and typed something else in. "Not in this state," he said. "Maybe he moved. I'll see what I can find out about Susanna."

"The mailman said something about his mail being sent on to a P.O. Box," I said.

"You could write him a letter then," Mom said. "Might make finding out the truth a lot easier."

The truth was that I really wanted there to be an invisible house behind that mailbox.

"So," Mom said, making her own breakfast, "what do you want to do for your birthday party? We're kind of running out of time to find a theme."

I shrugged. It wasn't like I had anyone here I knew well enough to invite, and I didn't even know how to get ahold of Victor and Lila again unless I ran into them. "Maybe we could do a gnome scavenger hunt."

"I like where your head's at, kiddo," Dad said. "Dive deeper into the secrets of the neighborhood."

"Do we have any stamps?" I asked.

Mom shook her head as she took a bite of her own peach bread. "I'll add that to the long list of groceries I need to pick up."

After I finished breakfast, I went to my backpack to find one of my old school notebooks. I tore out a blank page and went to the room I would share with Petals and imagined where my stuff would go. I sat on the floor, pretending to be on my bed.

Pulling off my pen's cap with my teeth, I started to write.

Dear Dr. Friedrich,

My name is Charlotte Jones and I just moved to this neighborhood. I found your mailbox and have so many questions. I'm sending you this note from someone who I think might be your daughter, so I thought you should have it. I hope this finds you well and that you will write me back.

Sincerely,
Charlotte Jones

I wondered why people always hoped a letter found others well and how that all got started as I put the letter and Susanna's note in one of the envelopes I had gotten from Dad's briefcase. I told my parents I would be right back.

Once more, I took off down the hill on my bike, this time more careful to not go too fast, and soon I was back at the empty lot.

I checked both ways for Otto the mailman, then pulled on the mailbox door. It was empty, but when the door opened, I heard a little 'ding.' Weird.

With the letter delivered, I decided I would go back and check on it over the next couple of days. If it was still there, I would admit defeat and mail it with a stamp so it could get sent on to his P.O. Box.

But, if it was gone, then I would know Dr. Friedrich must have picked it up himself.

On the way home, I stopped by the lending library and found an old copy of *Treasure Island*. I thought I might relate to someone who felt all alone somewhere new.

The old tire swing we had discovered in the backyard during last night's family movie game seemed like it would make a nice reading place, so I eased into it and started the first chapter.

I had completely lost myself in the story by the time Mom called for me, telling me I had mail.

"Who is it from?" I asked.

"Someone named Dr. Friedrich."

Six

I wanted to rip into the letter right away, but I stopped to look it over. The paper was smooth and cream colored. It felt expensive.

In the top left corner, it just said *D. Friedrich* without an address. In the middle of the envelope, the words *Charlotte Jones* and *Carefree Valley Drive* were in a pretty blue ink that he had written out by hand.

I narrowed my eyes at the stamp. It was the usual flag kind, but it shimmered in the light when I angled the envelope back and forth. The weirdest part, though, was that the postmark showed that it had been put in the mail yesterday.

That should not have been possible.

Carefully, I opened the top of the envelope and pulled out the fancy paper inside. It had a big, gold *F* stamped at the top and the words were written by a typewriter, but his name was signed in blue ink at the bottom.

Dear Charlotte,

I offer my sincere and true thank you for finding this note from Susanna and passing it along to me. If I may be so bold as to make a request, I would ask that any other notes you happen upon also be returned to my mailbox.

As a thank you and finder's fee, I am enclosing this 1976 $2 bill. It is worth more than it lets on, but only for those who know how to value it.

Yours truly,
Dr. Dieter Friedrich

My mind spun. This had to be a joke from Otto, right? He must have seen me put the letter in the mailbox, then typed up a reply, stamped it himself with yesterday's date, and then delivered it to my house.

It seemed like a lot of work for a joke.

I ran inside, holding the letter to my chest. Dad was working on his computer with headphones on, tapping his foot to some song I couldn't hear. I waved at him until he saw me.

"What's up, kiddo?"

"How much is a $2 bill from 1976 worth?"

He scrunched up his face. "Sorry," he said. "I don't think I know this riddle."

"No, really," I said. "Is it worth more than $2?" I nodded to his computer. "Could you check, please?"

"Oh, sure," Dad said, typing something into his laptop. "Why do you ask?"

"Can't a girl be curious?" I asked, giving him my most innocent shrug.

"Oh, you've always been a curious girl," Dad said. "That's what makes you fun." He scratched his chin and took off his glasses, leaning toward the screen. "It says a $2 bill from 1976 is worth about...$75."

My eyes went wide. I'd never had that much money before. The closest I had ever gotten was a $50 bond my grandma had given me that I couldn't cash in for years still. "Cool. Thanks!"

I spun around and ran out the front door before Dad could ask me any more questions.

It was time to do some gold digging. I mean, gnome house hunting.

I raced my bike down to the woods as fast as I could. As I got there, the birds chirped and tweeted all around, and I wished I knew their names just from their calls. I saw a bright red cardinal swoop low to another branch and I walked my bike down the trail to see it better.

I knew my mom loved red birds and it had something to do with where she grew up, or a baseball team or something. I kept my eyes open extra wide to catch any more flashes of red, but with the wind moving all of the leafy branches around, it looked like the whole sky danced above me.

Turning, I saw some red out of the corner of my eye. Only it wasn't a bird, and it wasn't moving. I walked off the trail and closer to a twisty old tree with a little red door filling in one of its knots.

I smiled. Maybe another message from Susanna waited for me inside.

With a tiny creaking noise, the door about the size of my fist opened up, and inside I saw a little metal object half buried in a pile of acorns.

Above, two angry squirrels let me know they were not happy I was getting into their secret stash of food. I reached in and pulled out the tiny metal thing. I remembered my mom would use one of these when she sewed.

A thimble, just like the one Wendy gave Peter Pan.

I swept the acorns aside, searching for a message, but I just got my hand dirty. So I tried to put the thimble on my pinky finger, but it wouldn't fit.

Something was inside it.

Carefully, I pulled out a scrap of paper and unfolded it a tiny drawing of a smiling fairy with curly hair. The artist had put their initials at the bottom.

S.F.

Susanna had been here after all. I wasn't sure if this would count to send to Dr. Friedrich or not, but I took the thimble and closed the door. I told the angry squirrels I was sorry, but it didn't seem to put them in a better mood.

I walked out of the woods and sat down next to my bike, dropping my backpack beside me. Fishing out my notebook, I wrote another letter:

Dear Dr. Friedrich,

Thank you for the generous reward. I found a small drawing in another gnome house and thought you might like it too. I am pretty sure Susanna drew the fairy.

I have to admit I am very curious about what happened to your house and why only a mailbox is there now. If you could tell me more about that, I would really appreciate it.

All the best,
Charlotte Jones

I sealed up my letter and the fairy drawing in another one of Dad's envelopes and put it into the mailbox. Once again, that ding sound happened and I closed it back up.

Since I didn't have any other plans for the day, I crossed the street and hid in the woods to see if Dr. Friedrich, or maybe even Otto, would show up and collect the mail.

I wished I had a pair of real spy glasses to see far away, but the best I could do was cup my hands around my eyes and wait. It felt like I had been there for hours, but my watch told me it had only been ten minutes. *How did people in stories have the patience to sit and wait for things to happen?*

"Hey!" a voice shouted behind me.

I nearly screamed in surprise, then turned around to see Victor and Lila walking down the forest path.

"Oh, hey," I said, heart racing. "You two scared me to death."

"Sorry," Lila said, scanning the area. "What's going on?"

I realized this seemed kind of weird but figured I should be honest. "I'm on a stakeout."

"Cool," Lila said. "Well, there's a snow cone truck back at the park and we saw you in the woods so I thought you might want to join us."

The only money I had on me was the $2 bill and no way was I spending it on a snow cone. But it felt nice being invited to something. One of the things I was most afraid of in coming to a new state was not making any friends.

I followed Lila and Victor through the forest, keeping my eyes open for any gnome houses but not mentioning it to them. I felt like I was making a friend in Susanna, and I liked only sharing that secret with Dad for now.

41

We got to the park and the snow cone truck reminded me of one we used to visit back at our old home. They had my favorite flavor here too: rainbow. I wondered how often the truck came to the park.

We walked over to the little lending library and filed through what was inside the bin.

"Hey," Victor said, "new books."

"Oooh!" Lila cried. "There are some good ones today!"

I stepped over to see a collection of classics with leather covers and gold stamped on their spines. It must have been somebody's special collection they kept in their library to try and seem really smart.

Robinson Crusoe went to Lila. Victor picked up *The Count of Monte Cristo* because he liked Monte Cristo sandwiches.

"This should count for like ten books towards a pizza," Victor said.

Then I noticed something at the bottom of the pile beneath *The Time Machine* by H.G. Wells.

A notebook.

I picked it up and flipped through the pages. It was a science journal with a lot of handwritten notes in the margins in blue ink. Most of it had something to do with light and transportation.

Then something slipped out of the back of the journal.

A set of blueprints.

House blueprints.

SEVEN

MY EYES WENT WIDE. *WHY WERE HOUSE BLUEPRINTS here?* I had found buried treasure and held it out for Victor and Lila to see.

"That's weird," Victor said, tucking his book under his arm.

"Maybe this is how he made his house disappear," I said to myself. I flipped to a page showing a science experiment about how to make something look invisible. There were even step-by-step instructions.

I knew what I would be doing with the rest of my day.

All I had to do was find baby oil, a glass bowl, and a clear drinking glass.

"What's light refr...refraction?" Lila asked, squinting at the page.

"I'm not sure," I said. "But I'm going to find out."

"Keep us posted," Victor said, chomping the last of his snow cone. "And let us know when you're having cake."

If I was going to be hunting for more secrets during my birthday party, I wanted to keep things to just my family. I gave an awkward smile, then raced home, pedaling as fast as I could. I was a sweaty mess by the time I got inside.

"Ah, perfect timing," Mom said.

The living room smelled a lot like wet paint. Usually I loved that smell, but I knew this time that meant I would have to help when there was science to be done.

Dad was on a small ladder painting the top part of the walls next to the ceiling that I couldn't reach. Petals had her own brush and was creating light blue smiley faces that would have to be covered over with a roller.

Mom handed me the roller.

I saw she wasn't wearing the usual painting clothes of one of Dad's old t-shirts.

"Aren't you painting too?" I asked.

She patted her belly. "Paint fumes aren't good for baby." She pointed to the wall Petals was playing on across the room. "Let's start with that one first, and please try not to get any paint on your sister. Dad will take over when he is done with the corners."

He turned his head. "I'm starting to think you only married me because of my height."

"Nonsense," Mom said. "There are always taller ladders. I picked you because you do such a great job not getting paint on the ceiling."

44

"I am pretty good at that," Dad said.

"We've got to get this done before the movers get here with our furniture." She picked up the keys to Oliver from the counter. "Anyone need something from the store?"

"Baby oil, please," I said, remembering the only ingredient from the science experiment.

Mom tilted her head to the side. "Baby boy isn't going to be here for a month."

"It's for a science experiment," I said.

"Hard to argue with science," Dad said, stretching to reach the ceiling. "Unless you're blowing something up. You're not blowing something up with science, are you, Chuckles?"

I shook my head.

"Okay," Mom said. "Wish me luck that the van comes back in one piece."

"His name is Oliver!" Petals said, then began painting a picture of our van.

With Mom gone, I started rolling paint, being extra careful not to get any on the floor or my clothes.

Dad had some fun music playing from his phone to help pass the time, but my mind kept drifting to the science journal and how that could be connected to the house blueprints.

"Rainbow!" Petals said, abandoning her post and running over to another section of the wall. "I'm gonna paint it."

I looked up and saw a bunch of colorful lights dancing around on the wall as the sun started to set outside.

The wind had picked up, knocking together Mom's crystal wind chimes she had already hung up on the front porch. She must have kept those separate from the rest of our stuff during the move so they wouldn't break.

Watching the light dance from the outside through those crystals and onto the wall reminded me of a picture in the science journal that I would have to check out when painting duty was over.

Somehow I managed to roll one wall without too many glops of light blue paint hitting the plastic sheet on the floor.

Dad finally finished his job on the ladder and took over for me, but not before offering to bribe Petals and me with a hidden stash of candy if we stuck around to keep painting.

Petals took him up on the offer, but I wanted to get to reading the journal. I ran back to my room.

Finally, I was free to dive back into the mystery.

Before long, I heard the front door open and the jingle of Mom's keys. "Movers are here!" she called.

"All hands on deck!" Dad shouted.

I gritted my teeth. Science would have to wait.

Eight

My job was mostly to not get squished by heavy furniture as I kept the doors open for the two big men who unloaded the moving truck. Petals stayed busy offering them warm bottles of water Mom had picked up from the store.

When nobody was looking, I grabbed the baby oil Mom had bought and snuck it off to my room. Next, I waited for any boxes marked 'Kitchen.'

The other two things I needed for the experiment were a large clear glass bowl, which I knew we had from when Mom would make punch at our birthday parties, and a small drinking glass.

It didn't take long for me to find what I needed since the movers brought the boxes right to the kitchen. With the bowl and small glass in my arms, I headed down the hall to my room.

"And where do you think you're going?" Dad asked, carrying what looked like a heavy box with 'Office' written on the side.

I really didn't want to lie. "Just a quick science experiment?"

Dad sighed, then shifted the box in his hands. "Family first, then science, okay kiddo?" He scooted past me in the hall on the way to his office, where he put the box down on his desk that looked kind of like an old airplane wing. "I know you're excited, but we all need to do our part right now. Team Jones, right?"

"Team Jones," I said, trying to stuff down how frustrated I felt. Finally there was something here that made moving stink less, and now I had to get back to the reminder that my life had been uprooted.

Two hours later, we lived in a maze of unpacked boxes. We ate leftover Chinese food that didn't taste as good as I remembered from last night on our old dining table and chairs.

After dinner, I excused myself to go back to my room. Even though I felt super tired, I still had enough energy to go and grab the book, flipping it to the invisibility experiment.

As I turned to the page, a small drawing fluttered out and onto the floor. It was the same drawing of the fairy I had found in the woods...

Didn't I just give that to Dr. Friedrich? What was it doing here?

It was yet another mystery I would have to unpack later. I looked at the blue cursive notes written all around the experiment trying to explain something called light refraction.

The writing looked like he was using a fountain pen. My dad loved writing with those too, and it made me think that maybe it would be fun to write my next letter back to Dr. Friedrich with one.

I grabbed the glass bowl I had put in my room and sat the drinking glass down inside of it.

Following the instructions, I poured the baby oil into the clear bowl, but outside of the glass.

So far, it just looked like a glass sitting in some liquid. Then the next step said to pour in more baby oil inside the drinking glass.

When the oil filled inside the glass, the bottom of it looked like it was beginning to disappear!

But I had completely run out of baby oil so I couldn't see it go fully invisible. The bottom of it was just a little bit harder to see. I had hoped the glass would completely disappear before my eyes.

Maybe in my next letter I could ask Dr. Friedrich if he could explain more about how this worked.

I suddenly got an idea. If I used my dad's fountain pen, maybe Dr. Friedrich would think we were kindred spirits and tell me everything about the house, too.

I remembered the box on Dad's desk, so I tiptoed out of my bedroom down to the office past Mom and Dad's room where they were busy unpacking some clothes.

Inside, I found a small box with Dad's pens and I pulled out one that was black but had etched lines all over it. I twisted the cap and saw the little diamond shaped tip that I thought I remembered Dad calling a nib.

He had warned me that you have to make sure not to put it down on the paper too hard or it could break the nib. Instead, you were supposed to just let it glide over the paper.

I sat the lid down on the desk next to the pen, then started to look for a clean sheet of paper to write on.

My heart sank when I heard the sound of rolling. The pen without the cap was perfectly round…and on its way off the side of Dad's desk!

I reached for it as it fell, but I was too slow.

The pen banged to the ground, landing right on the tip. I almost shouted, but I was afraid Dad would hear me.

When I picked it up off of the ground, I saw the nib had bent backwards. There was no way I could write with it.

Suddenly, what was going to be a letter about a science experiment had turned into a S.O.S. message to

the only other person I knew who used a fountain pen.
I grabbed a ballpoint pen and began to write.

Dear Dr. Friedrich,

I found your science journal and tried to make the glass disappear. It kind of worked, but I might need some help understanding what it has to do with refracting light and if it can really make something invisible.

I noticed you wrote your notes with a fountain pen, and I wanted to write you back with the one my dad has...but I kind of broke it. I hate to ask, but I could really use some help fixing it.

Tomorrow is my birthday and my only wish is to get this pen fixed before my dad finds out I messed it up.

Please help,
Charlotte Jones

NINE

AFTER FINISHING THE NOTE, I COULDN'T SLEEP A wink. As I tossed and turned, I remembered when Dad had first shown me his fountain pen and how it used to belong to his dad. If he found out, I don't know how long I would be grounded.

Or worse, he would just give me the sad look that meant I had really disappointed him. I kept having on and off nightmares about him giving me that look until daylight started to creep through my window.

I checked my watch. *6:15 a.m.* It would still be a while before everyone else got up. I wasn't excited about spending my whole birthday trying to keep the secret unless Dr. Friedrich could come through for me somehow.

Quietly, I eased out of my bed so I didn't wake up Petals. I put on an outfit and started learning which parts of the wood floor made the most noise when you stepped on them.

I carefully walked to my window and slid it up. It made a screech and I froze. Petals kept snoring, so I climbed out of the window with my letter and Dad's busted pen in an envelope.

I took off on my bike and headed down the hill into the morning mist. As I got to the mailbox, my walkie-talkie chirped to life. "Home Base to Chuckles, do you read? Please come in. Over." He sounded worried.

Busted. "I read you," I said, lifting the walkie-talkie. "Was just taking a morning ride. Over."

A long pause. I braced myself for getting in trouble. "All sorties need to be cleared with Mission Command."

"What's a sortie?" I asked as I put the envelope with Dad's pen into the mailbox. Opening it gave the familiar ding sound again. *What was with that?* The last letter I had left was gone, too.

"If you leave the house, we need you to tell us first," Dad said, not as playful as before. "You scared us when we couldn't find you anywhere."

"Sorry, Dad," I said. "Chuckles inbound. Over."

"Atta girl," Dad said. "Home Base will await the arrival of the birthday girl. Operation Secret Waffles is a go. Over and out."

I wanted to cry, but knew I would have to keep a brave face on while eating my all time favorite food for a special birthday breakfast.

I rode home and finished walking the bike up the hill. Petals was waiting by the front door, waving and jumping up and down. "We're eating waffles!" she said, then held a hand to her mouth and whispered loudly, "But it's a secret."

Patting her on the head as I walked by, I said, "Thanks for the warning."

As I stepped back inside, I saw papers taped together and marked with the light blue wall paint that said, H-A-P-P-Y-B-I-R-T-H-D-A-Y! I could tell Petals had made it since it had a smiley face on either side.

"Honey, you scared us so much," Mom said, walking up and giving me a hug.

"I'm sorry," I said, leaning into her. The hallway down to my room was filled with balloons and my doorway was covered in pink and purple streamers that I had missed because I snuck out the window.

Mom brought out a waffle with a lit candle in it. "We'll have cake later, but everybody knows making a wish on a birthday waffle makes it at least three to four times more likely to come true."

"We might need to check your sources on that," Dad said, putting his arm around Mom for a hug. "I heard it was more like 7 to 10 times."

I laughed a little bit. My family could be kind of goofy sometimes–well, a lot of the time–but it made me feel safe.

They sang the usual song, complete with Petals saying 'dear sister' instead of 'dear Charlotte.' I blew out the candle, not sure if I should wish for Dad's pen to be fixed or the answers to the mysteries of the invisible house.

But before I could get to my second bite of birthday waffle, a knock came at the door.

"Who could that be?" Mom asked, checking her watch.

Dad walked over to the door. "Birthday well-wishers?" He pulled it open.

Otto the mailman stood there in a blue bathrobe.

My heart raced. Did he already have the letter back from Dr. Friedrich with his magical timing? In his hand was my own envelope with Dad's pen still inside. My heart sank.

I slid off of my stool and rushed over to them to try and get the envelope before Otto could hand it to Dad.

"...and I'm sorry, but we can't keep having mail dropped off without a stamp on it like this," I heard Otto finish saying. "I live down the street from the mailbox and saw her put it in there." He turned to me. Then he saw the decorations.

"I mean...ah, happy birthday. But please, use postage next time. Actually..." He reached into his robe pocket and pulled out a small booklet of stamps. "Here you go. Got some spares. Happy birthday and feel free to send something all around the world next time."

I put my hand out for Otto to offer me the letter, but instead he gave it to Dad.

"Sorry about that," Dad said, taking the envelope and inspecting both sides. "We'll have a talk about it. And thanks for the stamps. Charlotte?" he asked, nodding to me.

"Oh, right. Sorry, Mr. Otto," I said. I didn't say I wouldn't try to write Dr. Friedrich again, but I knew I was going to have to be trickier about not getting caught.

Otto nodded, then left. Dad closed the door and felt the envelope. "What did you send him this morning? I thought you were just out for a ride." He began to open the letter and let the contents slide out into his hand.

But it wasn't a pen that slid out.

It was a glass rod, perfectly smooth and about the same size as Dad's fountain pen.

"Well, I can see why you wouldn't want to mail this," Dad said. "But what is it?"

A small note fluttered out of the envelope and I scooped it up quickly. It was a handwritten message from Dr. Friedrich. I picked it up and skimmed it but would have to read it later.

"I was trying to do a science project that I found in a book from the lending library. That's why I needed the baby oil and glass." I glanced down at the note again. He must have given me this piece of glass to try with the experiment.

"Huh," Dad said. "Well, best not to make our neighbors mad or let our waffles get cold, eh, kiddo?" He smiled and I took a deep sigh of relief.

I went back to my stool at the kitchen island and took another bite of my breakfast, then read the note while it sat on my lap.

> *Dear Charlotte,*
>
> *I am delighted you tried my experiment on light refraction. I am enclosing a solid glass rod for you to do a second experiment with. I believe you will find more success with it than a common drinking glass.*
>
> *Your father's pen injury is a right tragedy. However, I am familiar with the model and shall send it to the nibsmith who services my own writing instruments. It shall take some time, and I will consider the collection of another one of Susanna's notes as full payment.*
>
> *Happy Birthday,*
> *Dieter Friedrich*

After I finished eating, I went back to my room, kicking up a bunch of the balloons filling the hallway.

I ducked beneath the birthday streamers on my doorway and saw an outfit laying on my bed I hadn't seen before.

A plain red shirt and blue shorts sat next to a pointy red hat.

It was a gnome outfit.

"No way," I said.

I turned around and saw my family all wearing matching gnome outfits.

"Let's go gnome house hunting!" Mom said.

TEN

"PLEASE DON'T MAKE ME WEAR THIS," I SAID, pointing to the gnome outfit on my bed.

"But it's so cute!" Mom protested.

"So cute! Squawk!" Petals, who was now a parrot or something, said.

I leaned over and picked up the pointy felt hat. It looked like Mom had made it herself. I didn't want to make her sad, so I put it on, tucking the strap beneath my chin. She lifted her phone and I held up a hand.

"No pictures posted anywhere," I said. "Please?"

Mom took a deep breath and breathed out 'fine' through her teeth as she put her phone down. She walked out of the room and I thought I heard her say something about 'senior yearbook blackmail.'

I got changed and gave a short presentation in the living room of my new outfit, complete with a twirl.

"So, is the gnome hunt going to be a race or something?" I asked.

"We could split up into teams," Dad said.

"I pick Mommy," Petals said, rushing over to grab Mom's leg. "Squawk."

Dad glanced over at me. "You good with that, kiddo?"

I nodded. Petals would probably just wind up picking flowers anyway, and Mom wasn't going to be climbing any trees to hunt for gnome houses.

We left the house and I checked to see if anyone would spot me in my pointy hat. We took Oliver down the hill so Mom wouldn't have to make the hike back to the house. Dad parked next to the mailbox and we all piled out of the van and headed into the woods in our matching outfits.

Right away, Petals ran off from the trail, shouting "Flowers!"

Mom followed her and waved bye to me as she tried to keep up.

"I'm thinking we might win," Dad said, adjusting the strap on his hat. "But at least we all get cake." He patted me on the shoulder. "That's the important part, right?"

"Who do you think made these gnome houses?" I asked, trying to keep a lookout for anything that didn't belong in the forest.

"Probably someone who lives around here," Dad said. "And has a lot of time on their hands."

"And someone who loves gnomes," I added, watching a pair of squirrels chatter angrily with each other over something. I wondered if they were the same ones from when I found Susanna's fairy artwork.

"Maybe," Dad said. "Or they could be making the houses for someone who loves gnomes."

"Like Susanna," I said. I thought it was a little bit odd that she was the only one who had left messages. Since the notes were so old, I had to imagine that nobody else had found these gnome houses except her for years and years.

I watched the light coming through the tree branches, wondering if Susanna liked to climb and if more of the notes were up there. Two gray and black birds danced around with each other, fighting over a worm. "Dad, what kind of birds do you think those are?"

"Wish I could remember," he said. "When I was your age, I was in Scouts and knew every type of bird and tree in this forest. Now I'm not even sure how to search for that."

We walked farther away from the path and into a grove of trees. I could faintly hear Petals giggling but couldn't see where she or Mom had gone. The trees gave way into a small field with a pond at its center.

The sound of the flying machine caused me to crane my neck and see Mr. Adams making another trip around the forest. I waved at him but he couldn't see me. He disappeared behind the branches and my eyes were drawn to a splash of color up above in the trees.

"Dad, how about you look low and I look high?" I asked. "But first can you give me a boost into this tree?"

I could tell Dad was trying to decide how likely it was I'd wind up with a broken arm or leg on my birthday. "Do you see something?"

"I think so," I said, trying to get a grip on the bark of the thick trunk. My arms weren't long enough to wrap around it to pull myself up, but there was a low-hanging branch I could use to climb to the top if I had a little help.

Dad came over and picked me up. It reminded me of how he used to lift me so I could put the angel on the top of our Christmas tree as our tradition, but now Petals had the honor since she was littler.

With a grunt, Dad got me up where I needed to go. "Make sure your shoes stay tied."

I balanced by keeping a hand on the trunk to keep myself from falling. From there I was able to grab onto the other limbs and climb the tree like a ladder.

Below, Dad seemed a lot smaller, and I started to wonder if being this high up was such a good idea. I was suddenly very glad Dad hadn't decided to go off and search for other gnome houses by himself.

Once I almost reached the top of the tree, I found the little bit of color that had caught my eye. It was a scrap of pink paper that had been used to help build a nest.

A nest full of baby birds.

Who had a bird mommy.

A bird mommy who wasn't too happy that a giant gnome girl had climbed all the way up to her home to scare her babies.

"Sorry," I whispered to the bird family. The chirps did not sound like they thought it was okay that I was still here. Another bird landed on the limb, made an angry squawk, then flew away.

I watched where it landed, over on a big stump near the edge of the field. It disappeared inside, then returned with another pink scrap of paper.

"That's weird," I said, then watched the bird come flying in right at my head. "Oh no!" I yelled, losing my grip on the branch as I ducked to avoid being hit by the flapping wings.

"Charlotte!" Dad shouted.

I fell down a branch, but one of the limbs caught on the crook of my elbow and kept me from falling all the way down. It hurt so badly as I jerked to a stop.

"I'm okay," I said, not really sure that was true.

My heart beat so loudly I could hear it in my ears and I felt shaky. I carefully started my way down but started to slip again.

Just then, I felt something wrap around my right leg. *Dad*. He grabbed me just as I was about to fall, pulling me into his arms.

He carefully carried me down safely to the ground. I dug my head into his chest and tried not to cry.

"I'm sorry," I said.

"It's okay," Dad said. "How about I take the low road and you take the low road too, huh?"

That sounded like a great idea. It took me a few moments to calm down.

"Did you see anything?" Dad asked.

I had almost forgotten about the stump the bird had found the colorful paper in. I pointed to the edge of the field. "There's something over there," I said. My hand still shook when I pointed.

Dad patted me on the shoulder and we walked through the tall grass over to the giant stump. As we got close to it, I could see that the top of it actually looked more like a wooden lid than part of a dead tree. There was even a small hole where the bird had snuck through.

"Well, that's odd," Dad said, poking a thumb through the place where the bird got in and out. He gave the top of the stump a lift. A perfect circle came up like it was a lid, and he sat it down next to the edge of the stump.

Down the hole, a small ladder led into the dark. "What on earth," I said under my breath.

Dad's eyes were wide with excitement. "What did you find?"

Eleven

DAD SHINED HIS PHONE'S FLASHLIGHT INTO THE hole to reveal a colorful world below. Old pillows, blankets, and books in every color of the rainbow sat along the walls of the small dug out cave.

"I think we found the biggest gnome house ever," I said.

"Hold on," Dad said, shining his light around several more times. "Let me make sure there aren't any snakes or something down here." He swung his leg over the side and climbed down the ladder.

"Good plan," I said. "I like that plan." Snakes were one of my least favorite things ever. And ladybugs, but I still wasn't sure why those creeped me out as much as they did.

I wondered how everything didn't get soaked down there when it rained, but then I saw the circular lid of the stump had a rubber ring around the edge of it to seal it to the stump top. *Who made this?*

"Coast is clear," Dad called up, shining his light onto the ladder so I could see where I was climbing down. "You're not going to believe this."

As I made my way into the life-sized gnome house, the floor was only far enough down that I could stand and not hit my gnome hat on the ceiling, but Dad had to crouch.

He shined his light on me and I held my hand up to block it.

"Sorry," he said, moving the light down. "Check this out." He gave a slow tour of the hideout.

Hand drawn paintings and sketches of unicorns, fairies, and gnomes were attached to cork boards on the walls. I could tell the artist right away from her style. *Susanna.*

In the corner sat a small bookshelf with old paperback novels, mostly detective and science fiction books with well-worn cracked spines. Next to the shelf were a half dozen colorful pillows to make a cozy reading nook and an old, black flashlight she must have used when she spent time down here.

I walked over and picked up the flashlight. It was super heavy, and when I pressed the rubbery button, it clicked but no light shone. The batteries must have died a long time ago.

"Well, if you ever wanted to know where all of the gnome houses were, I've got some spoilers for you," Dad said, pointing his light on a map taped to another board.

Polaroid photos of each gnome house were pinned down with a date written below each picture in pink paper.

A few of the scraps of paper were gone, and I knew they were now a part of the bird's nest. The ones that were still there were labeled with a date in the 1960s that I guessed matched when each one had been found.

As I took a step forward, I tripped on something and stumbled into Dad. He turned around and caught me. "You okay?" he asked.

"Yeah, I'm fine," I said, then turned around to see what my foot had caught on. I knelt down and felt a metal handle sticking out from the ground.

Was there another hidden level to this place?

I gave the handle a tug, and a small circular lid came up out of the ground. Buried in the dirt floor was the rest of a metal cooking pot.

Inside, a small package was neatly bundled in some rainbow colored cloth. I carefully picked it up and Dad shined his light on my hands.

The bundle had a small bit of string tied around it, so I untied it. The cloth unfolded in my hand and I found myself staring at a beautiful glass unicorn.

It must have been a prized possession Susanna had left here. But why would she not remember to take something like this with her if she eventually moved out of this neighborhood?

I wanted to give it to her, but started to wonder if Susanna was still alive today.

At least I knew someone I could ask about it.

I gently rewrapped the glass unicorn. "I want to give this to Dr. Friedrich," I said. "I think he would like it." I wasn't really thinking about another $2 bill, but more that if Dr. Friedrich had sent me that glass rod, then this was something he might have given Susanna, and he wouldn't want it lost in the woods.

Dad took pictures of everything, especially the map of all of the gnome houses. "Hey, look," he said, pointing to one gnome house that was outside of the forest and far away from the rest of them. "That one might be somewhere around our house. That's weird." He smiled at me. "I'd say this was a successful birthday adventure. We probably won the scavenger hunt, don't you think?"

I laughed. "Unless Petals found an even bigger cave."

We climbed out and carefully put the lid of the stump back just right so it would keep rain out.

With the sun rising higher in the sky, the day had started to warm up a lot. We found Mom sitting in the shade on a downed tree log, watching Petals pick dandelions on the other side of the field.

Dad showed her the pictures he took and Mom seemed really impressed.

69

"And there were no snakes in there, right?" she asked.

"First thing we checked," I said. "Well, Dad checked."

"Then we'll have to all go next time we take a family adventure," she said, holding out her hand for Dad to help her up.

Before we headed back to the house in Oliver, I glanced both ways to make sure Otto wasn't around, then placed the glass unicorn in Dr. Friedrich's mailbox. We all piled into the van and headed up the hill for some morning birthday cake.

But when we arrived at the house, a package was waiting on the front porch with my name on it. "I'm not sure how mail even works in this neighborhood anymore," Dad said as he picked it up. "It's from…Germany? Who do you know in Germany?"

I shrugged and took the package from Dad. Running inside, I found one of the kitchen knives to cut open the tape.

The box contained a note and two fountain pens. The first one was Dad's, and I quickly tucked that into my pocket before anyone could see it.

Opening the folded note, I saw that it had the familiar golden *F* at the top, so I knew who had sent it right away. But what was he doing in Germany?

Dear Charlotte,

I hope you are having the most wonderful of birthdays. I know I am enjoying myself on account of your most thoughtful of deliveries. I thought I would never see the glass unicorn again, and it does my heart good to behold it once more.

Enclosed, you will find your father's pen, repaired and left better than it was found. My man Harley gave it a good cleaning and it should work as well as when it was originally purchased.

I am also adding in a pen for yourself. It will write quite well, but please do see to it that you take good care of it as it should last you a lifetime.

As a final birthday present, I believe I have done a most terrible job of confusing you with the nature of my deliveries and the property I own in your neighborhood.

If you are available between 7:00 and 7:05 this evening, I should like to explain things to you in person about what I have been working on.

Best wishes,
Dieter

TWELVE

THIS WAS IT. I WAS FINALLY GOING TO GET MY ANSWERS. All of them.

Well, five minutes' worth of answers. *Why only five minutes?* And how had he sent a letter from Germany saying he had gotten the glass unicorn when I had just dropped it off a few minutes ago?

My mind spun, and I must have had a goofy look on my face when I stopped daydreaming because Dad was waving his hand, saying, "Yoohoo, Earth to Charlotte. You with us?"

"Sorry," I said, shaking my head to snap out of it. I held up my new silver and black fountain pen. It was the same brand as my grandpa's. "Look what I got from Dr. Friedrich in the mail."

Mom walked up to check out the birthday present. "Oh wow, looks like you have a pen pal now," she said, then laughed. "Get it? *Pen* pal?"

"No, no, I get it," I said.

"Everyone talks about dad jokes," Mom said as she handed the pen to Dad. "Nobody gives the ladies any love for bad puns too."

"You get points in my book," Dad said as he inspected the pen. He turned it over in his hand, then unscrewed the cap and checked out the nib. "Oh, wow," he said. "24 karat gold nib. These things aren't cheap. I'll have to show you how to write with it without breaking it. That's, uh…a really nice gift."

He gave a look over to Mom. I could tell they were trying to talk to each other without using words. Years ago, they had to stop spelling things in front of me when I learned to read, so now all they had left were long looks where they opened their eyes really wide and raised and lowered their eyebrows like it was some sort of secret code I wasn't supposed to crack.

"What's wrong?" I asked. "Something is up."

"Honey," Dad said, turning to me. "How well do you know Dr. Friedrich?"

It was a good question. I guess I had gotten so carried away with the mystery of it all that I hadn't stopped to think if any of this was a good idea.

Ever since Dad had told us we were going to have to move again, I had been so sad and didn't want to leave my friends and school.

Even when I tried so hard to make friends, only one or two had stuck around, and nobody had even tried to call me since we left. I was starting to feel like I had been forgotten, and then suddenly there was this fun mystery and someone who would actually write to me.

I shrugged. "He seems nice from the letters."

"Maybe we should be a little extra careful about it until Mom and I can meet him," Dad said, handing me back the pen.

"We just want you to be safe," Mom added.

"So, new rule," Dad said. "No going down to that mailbox without getting an okay from us or we have to go down there with you. Sound good?"

I sighed. Here I was with a chance to finally get my answers and they didn't trust that it would be safe to go.

But it made sense. I had been taught never to go into a stranger's car, and meeting up with an adult I didn't know could be even worse.

I bit my lip and came up with a plan. "Can we at least print off the pictures you took of the cave and I can drop them off at his mailbox with you after dinner? It wouldn't take long. Like only five minutes. Maybe at seven o'clock? And when we come back we could open presents then."

Mom and Dad gave each other another look.

"He just seems to check his mail a lot, and I bet if we saw him down there, then you could meet him," I said.

"We've taken a lot of trips down there already–"

"What would Sherlock Dad do?" I asked.

Mom glanced over at the kitchen table, then did a double take. "Petals, no!" She ran over to stop my little sister from grabbing a second fist-full of cake.

"It was just his hat!" Petals said, her fingers and mouth red with frosting from the gnome shaped cake Mom had made. "You're not 'posed to wear a hat inside. Right?" She gave her best icing-covered grin.

I ran over to grab some napkins and helped Mom clean up Petals.

"Sorry, sister," Petals said. "His hat was so yummy and my hat wasn't, so I wanted to trade."

"It's okay," I said, trying not to laugh at how the cake now was just an old man who wore suspenders. Actually, he kind of looked like Santa if the jolly old guy wore blue pants instead of red. "It can be my Christmas in July cake."

We all had a slice, then Dad tapped me on the shoulder. "Sherlock Dad and Chuckles will be on the case," he said with a smile. "I'll get the printer unpacked."

I got changed into my favorite purple shirt with a unicorn printed on it and some pink shorts, then spent the rest of the afternoon searching the science project book and reading Dr. Friedrich's notes.

Dad took a break from unpacking to show me how to hold my fountain pen and made up a practice sheet with all of the cursive letters for me to try to match as best I could. I had to hold the pen just right for the ink to flow on the page and I was extra careful to not press too hard to bend the tip of it.

I practiced tracing Dr. Friedrich's cursive notes and tried to understand how the solar panels on the roof in the house blueprints had anything to do with the speed of light he kept talking about in the science journal. I knew light travelled to us that fast from the sun, but that was all I could figure out.

In my best penmanship, I wrote my list of questions to ask Dr. Friedrich since I would only have a little bit of time.

Questions for Dr. Friedrich
1. What happened to your house?
2. How do you get mail delivered so fast?
3. Does Susanna still like gnomes?
4. Where did the gnome houses come from?

Soon dinner came. Mom had made my favorite spaghetti bake recipe and we had the leftover Santa

Gnome boot cake while Dad finished printing off the photos for us to deliver.

I checked my watch. It was already 6:50. Mom had to wrestle down a sugar-hyper Petals, who now said she was a puppy, to get her into the bath while I took the folder of photos and put them into my backpack.

"Can we take Oliver?" I asked. "I'd rather not get sweaty again on my way back up."

"But that's half the fun," Dad said, taking the keys off of the kitchen counter and tossing them to me. "Fine. You're driving."

"I'm eleven!"

"Oh, right," Dad said with a wink. "Wrong birthday. What was I thinking?" He playfully grabbed the keys back and strapped on his gnome hat. "What do you think? Should we give this another spin?"

"It makes you look taller," I said.

He took off the pointy cone. "If I get any taller, Mom is going to ask me to start painting the outside of the house, and as you've discovered, we Joneses aren't known for balancing in high places." He touched my elbow. "That still hurt?"

A bruise had started to form and I covered it up with my hand. "A little."

Dad patted me on the shoulder. "I'm sure the other kids will think it is cool."

We walked out to Oliver and climbed in, then took the three minute drive down to Dr. Friedrich's mailbox.

Rounding the corner, I almost missed it because this time it blended in with the rest of the mailboxes.

Because this time, there was a house behind it.

Thirteen

I couldn't believe it! All of my crazy hopes that there was an invisible house were right! Although, I guess it wasn't an invisible house anymore.

"You're seeing this too, right?" I asked.

Dad just stared ahead as he turned the keys to stop Oliver. "…yeah." He held out his phone and took a picture.

I tried not to be worried that Dr. Friedrich wasn't anywhere outside. The clock on Oliver's dashboard said 6:59 p.m. I checked my own watch and it said 7:04.

"Dad, I think we're late!"

"Late for what?"

I swung open my door, checked both ways down the street and ran across to the mailbox.

"Charlotte, wait!"

"Hello?" I called. "Dr. Fried–"

As soon as I stepped past the mailbox, everything went silent around me.

No bird calls, no chirps from bugs or frogs, and even the wind rushing through the trees and bushes had stopped. I turned to look at Dad, who was frozen in place, stuck while climbing out of the driver's seat.

"Dad!" I called out, but my own voice sounded like I was inside some sort of bubble with the house. I walked toward him but hit an invisible wall and fell backwards onto the ground.

Then, breaking the silence, a really creepy sound came from the house. The solar panels on the roof started to glow orange, then a neon blue. I turned my head so I wouldn't be blinded by the bright light.

"Help!" I shouted, searching for some way to escape. Out of the corner of my eye, I noticed the trees were starting to move funny. Not only were they shaking quickly, but beneath them I saw a version of myself running backwards and getting back into Oliver, then our van drove away in reverse the way we had come.

The sky then started to grow brighter as the sun began to peek back up above the trees.

None of this should be possible.

Not only was the sun peeking back up, but it started rising higher into the sky. More cars passed by, also driving backwards in the neighborhood, and I could even see Victor and Lila riding their bikes backwards for a moment!

By the time the sun had quickly crossed the sky to the other side, I could see Oliver parked on the street from my morning birthday gnome hunt, and there was my own family and me getting out of the van and walking backwards into the woods!

I was going backward in time.

As I watched in disbelief, things started to speed up. My family and the earlier version of me returned to Oliver and reversed down the street. Soon it was night and the moon flew up fast enough that it looked like a white streak, which then turned into a golden streak as the sun took its turn.

Back and forth they traded places until they became two lines across the sky, and anything that moved on the street was a complete blur.

The leaves began to shrink back into the trees and the air grew cold as snow appeared around me and then was sucked back into the sky, over and over. Seasons were changing. I ran to the front porch of Dr. Friedrich's house.

My heart pounded in my chest as the world spun in reverse, and I wondered how far back we were going…and how I could get home.

The strobing lights became too much for me to take, so I tried the front door handle and found it was unlocked. Twisting the knob, I ran inside and tripped over my own feet and landed in the entryway.

Turning around, I put my back to the door and shut it with my shoulder. This all had to be a really bad dream.

As the lights flickered from day to night and back again through the front windows, I tried to take in the foyer of the house. Right in front of me were wooden stairs, and next to them was a long hallway that led down to a kitchen.

I knew the house blueprints inside and out at this point. It was the same place.

On the wall next to me I saw a family portrait of three people, none of them smiling. A mother who seemed like she was trying not to frown, the father who wore wire-rimmed glasses and was starting to go bald on top, and a girl who was about my age. She wore a pretty purple dress and had a matching band in her long, dark hair.

This had to be the Friedrich family. I was finally getting to see Susanna and her parents.

Did they all live here? If this house could travel through time, it might have made sense with all of the old dates on the notes from the gnome houses. What if they all lived in the past and made the trip to the future from time to time to explore or answer the letters of a curious girl?

Down the flowery wallpaper-covered hallway, a humming sound of a machine running caught my attention as the buzzing noise came through a cracked open door. Blue lights flickered into the hallway and I built up the courage to go and check it out.

I crept up to the door and saw it led down a flight of stairs to a basement. I noticed there were wires like the ones in the blueprint leading from the roof down beneath the house. The roof's solar panels had been powering something down below.

Suddenly, with a loud snap, the flickering of lights from the sun and the moon stopped, leaving sunlight shining in through the front windows.

Starting to feel really homesick, I walked over to the basement door. If Dr. Friedrich was down there, maybe he could help me get back to my family.

Even though I shook with nervousness, I took the first step down and kept one foot in front of the other until I could see fully into the basement.

A very large machine took up most of the room and it felt very warm down here, which was probably from the heat the machine had made from working so hard to send the house back in time.

Along the wall hung several white lab coats, but nobody to wear one. As I took a step farther into the room, I saw a series of photos hanging up on the wall…pictures of Susanna from far away as she was playing with the gnome houses.

Someone had been spying on her.
But then I noticed something.
The last picture on the wall was of me.

Fourteen

I FROZE. WHY DID DR. FRIEDRICH HAVE A PICTURE of me when I was finding one of the gnome houses? Had he been spying on me? My heart began to race and I felt less safe than ever.

I looked through the timeline of photos of Susanna, each of them discovering one of the gnome houses, and they had different dates written beneath them.

At the end of the row of eight pictures, there was a blank space for a photo to go. Beneath it, the date of July 13, 1968 was written.

Just beyond the machine in the middle of the room there was a workbench, only instead of science experiment tools, I saw…crafting supplies?

Dr. Friedrich had been working on building something with a white circular base and a big red dome next to it. Maybe this was going to be the next gnome house, but one that looked like a mushroom.

Then it hit me. Dr. Friedrich was the one making all of the gnome houses.

I walked closer to check it out, first glancing over my shoulder to make sure Dr. Friedrich wasn't coming down the stairs. Now that the machine had gotten quiet, I felt like I needed to hold my breath so I wouldn't make much noise, and I tiptoed over to the wooden workbench to check out the gnome house in progress.

Inside the base of the mushroom were three glass figures of fairies all sitting together, enjoying tea. Two sat on a little fairy couch and another lay on the floor playing with something that looked like a fairy version of a cat.

When I had found the gnome houses, they were just filled with Susanna's notes, not glass figurines, but it made sense that if Susanna had found these first then she would have taken them with her.

Clank. I heard the door at the top of the stairs open. Someone muttered a frustration that it had been left ajar and that the girl from the neighborhood had never shown up.

I didn't know what to do, so I searched for somewhere I could hide. There was space under the table with all of the crafting supplies and it went far back enough that as long as he didn't need any of the paints or anything else beneath it, he shouldn't be able to spot me.

Before I could see more than just his knees coming down the stairs, I quickly and quietly climbed below the table, careful not to push over any of the paint cans there.

The footsteps got closer and I tried to be as still as possible as he walked up to the desk. He stood there for a really long time, humming some song I didn't know, and then his hand reached down beneath the table, almost grabbing my leg!

Instead he wrapped his hand around a small can of white paint and didn't seem to notice that I had pulled my leg further back. I tried to breathe a sigh of relief as quietly as I could. My heart pounded in my ears so loud it felt like anyone could hear it.

After a few moments, I heard him say, "There we are." His voice sounded old and kind of weak. I heard him grunt as the mushroom gnome house scraped against the top of the table, then he struggled to carry it away and up the stairs.

I shook as I waited to hear the sound of the front door open and shut. I counted to ten, then felt like I was safe to come out from my hiding spot.

Whether I liked it or not, I needed answers and I needed to find a way home. I thought about whether or not I could figure out how to work the time machine, but when I got up and checked it out, none of the controls made sense to me. I really didn't want to wind up a million years in the future or something.

I was scared to actually talk to Dr. Friedrich all on my own, but I knew I had to be brave if I wanted to see my family again. I carefully walked up the stairs to the front door and tried the handle.

It was locked, even though doors shouldn't lock from the inside...I tried to undo the deadbolt, but as soon as I put my fingers on the knob, a voice called out to me from the speaker next to the door.

"*Identification,*" the machine said.

"Uh...can I get out please?"

"*Identification.*"

"...Charlotte Jones?"

"*Invalid,*" the machine said. "*One more failed attempt and full lockdown will begin.*"

I took a deep breath, noticing the clock on the wall. It said it was 10:35 a.m. so I adjusted my watch while I gave some thought as to how to answer the door computer. I would have to make the next guess good. I looked around until I saw the family picture by the door. "Susanna. Susanna Friedrich."

The machine took a moment longer than I would have liked to reply.

"*Proceed, Susanna.*" The deadbolt twisted on its own and unlocked. "*And please do not joke about being Charlotte Jones again. That name is not allowed access at this point in the timeline.*"

88

Having no idea what that meant, I opened the door just in time to see a man with white hair carrying the mushroom house into the woods.

Immediately something smacked me in the face and I let out a little yelp as I threw my hands up to protect myself.

A boy on a bike rode by and yelled, "Sorry!"

At my feet was a newspaper he had just thrown. Bending down, I picked up the paper and saw the date on it: *Saturday, July 13, 1968.*

My eyes went wide. I took off, dashing down the porch steps and onto the front yard.

Passing the mailbox, I gave it a glare for getting me into all of this trouble in the first place.

A car horn honked as it drove by, almost hitting me. I gave an 'I'm sorry' wave but still got the stink eye from the man driving the car.

He pointed a finger at me and shouted. "Watch yourself! Kids today..."

The baby blue car drove by, and Dr. Friedrich had disappeared into the woods. Suddenly, I had an idea. I opened my backpack and found the folder with the printed off pictures of Susanna's gnome house map. As I carefully crossed the street, I looked down to try to see which location had the new mushroom one.

I couldn't spot it in any of the forest pictures, so I just ran forward on the trail and tried to do my best to track along until I heard the huffing and puffing of an old man carrying something too heavy for him.

It didn't take too long to spot Dr. Friedrich, and by the time I had gotten close enough to get his attention, another voice beat me to it.

"Hey!" the voice of a young woman shouted. "It's you!"

Dr. Friedrich looked up in a panic to see a young woman about my age with long, dark hair wearing a light purple sundress. *Susanna.* He dropped the gnome house and it fell on its side with a crash. I cringed as I imagined the glass figures breaking inside.

Then he bolted faster than I've ever seen someone his age run.

"Wait!" I shouted, my voice matching the word the other girl had said at the exact same time. We stared at each other for a moment in confusion. It was definitely Susanna.

Without another moment to spare, we both started chasing after Dr. Friedrich through the trails. I liked to think I was pretty fast for my age, but I couldn't keep up with my backpack bouncing side to side when I tried to run up the trail.

"Do you know who that is?" Susanna called out to me.

"Oh, no," I said, realizing that Dr. Friedrich was running back to his house. I saw an orange light flash through the trees, then blue. A loud whining sound shook the trees. "No, no, no!"

We both came out the other side of the woods and stared at the lot with nothing but a mailbox on it.

It was official.

I was stuck in 1968.

FIFTEEN

ALL I COULD DO WAS STARE AT THE EMPTY LOT where Dr. Friedrich's house had stood. I wanted to scream and cry all at once, but I felt so numb that I couldn't do either.

"Where did he go? Did you know him?" Susanna said as she turned around, eyes wide.

I shook my head and felt a tear drip down my cheek.

"Hey, are you okay?" Susanna asked, taking a step toward me.

I didn't know what I could say to this past version of Susanna. So many time travel stories talk about not spoiling the future for people in the past...not that I knew much about her other than she put notes in gnome houses her father from the future left for her in the woods.

But then I got an idea. What if the version of Susanna's dad from 1968 could help me get back to my own time?

"What's your name?" Susanna asked. I could tell she was trying not to say anything about how I was dressed. My purple unicorn shirt, pink shorts, and sparkly tennis shoes were decades out of place.

"Charlotte," I said.

Susanna walked over to me and put an arm around my shoulder to try to make me feel better. She was a few inches taller and was probably just about to start high school. "Are you lost?"

"Yeah, a little," I said, following Susanna down the sidewalk and using a sleeve to wipe my cheeks.

"Let's go back to my house and see if we can call your parents," Susanna said. She kept shifting her eyes back to the empty lot. "I really thought I was going to catch him this time," she said. "Must have had a car waiting or something."

"That would make sense," I said. I wondered how much she knew about the man who built the gnome houses, so I decided to tiptoe around the topic. "What were you doing in the forest?"

Susanna stopped. "What were *you* doing in the forest?"

"I saw that guy carrying that giant mushroom thing, so I decided to follow him."

"Have you ever seen him before?" Susanna asked.

"First time," I said. "Weird that he would be carrying something like that, huh?"

"Yeah," Susanna said, not adding anything else. I understood why she would want to keep her gnome houses private. They were probably a special secret she thought was just for her. "Actually, he kind of reminded me of photos of my grandpa."

"Really?"

"Yeah, but my grandpa died in the second World War."

"Oh, I'm sorry to hear that," I said.

I looked up to see the hill where my house should have been and saw only Mr. Adams's house there. Where I lived probably wasn't going to be built for a while, so I couldn't exactly walk up to the previous owners and ask them to deliver a message into the future to tell Dad what had happened and to have Dr. Friedrich come back for me.

But what if I could ask Dr. Friedrich himself to do that? Well, that would mean he would have known I had gone back in time with him and he would have left me here anyway.

Thinking through all of this was so tiring.

"So, what school do you go to?" Susanna asked.

I tried to remember the name of the school I was supposed to start in once summer break ended, but Mom had only said the name once and I couldn't remember it. Plus, even if I knew the name, it might not have even been built yet.

The last thing I wanted was to get caught in a lie and sound crazy. "We just moved here," I said, taking the easy route. "I'm not sure."

"Oh, that makes sense since I've never seen you around before...ah, here we are," Susanna said as we approached her house. It was pretty much the same as the time traveling one, only it didn't have the solar panels on the roof. "Okay, can you wait on the porch while I talk to my mom?"

"Sure," I said.

Susanna let herself in with a key she had hanging around her neck and disappeared for a minute while I waited. I took a moment to go through my backpack and pulled out the photos of the different locations of the gnome houses. I tried to memorize as many of them as I could, but then, as I heard footsteps coming back to the door, I quickly stuffed the folder back into my bag and zipped it up.

"Come in," Susanna said, waving me inside.

Stepping into the house felt so weird because the family picture of the three Friedrichs hung in the same place as the time traveling house. Even the same flowery wallpaper was on the hallway walls.

It felt like a tease that I had just left this place but this version of it couldn't take me back home.

I guessed Dr. Friedrich didn't figure out time travel until 1983 if Mr. Adams's photos could be believed.

As Susanna led me toward the kitchen, I could hear sounds coming from down below in the basement.

"Is your dad here?" I asked.

Susanna nodded. "Yes, but we can't bother him," she said quietly. "When he's busy, he gets super mad if he's interrupted." She pointed to a bare light bulb that glowed red above the basement door. "When that's on, if I even call down to him I get grounded."

"Oh," I said. I didn't want to get Susanna in trouble, but I really needed to talk to her dad so I could get home.

We walked softly past the basement entrance to the kitchen, where I saw the tall and lean, serious looking woman from the family photo.

She stood behind her kitchen counter and her eyes ran me up and down. I really wished I had been wearing something different because I could tell that how I dressed was confusing to her.

"Susanna tells me you're lost," Mrs. Friedrich said. "You are welcome to use our phone to call your parents if they are local. Otherwise, I'm afraid I will have to ask you to call collect."

She pointed to a really old phone that had a bunch of numbers in a circle that I had zero idea how to use. And what did 'calling collect' even mean?

A white, fluffy cat rubbed against my leg.

"Weena, no, girl," Susanna said, picking up the cat so that her hands disappeared in its stomach fluff. "I'm sorry, are you allergic?"

I reached over and gave Weena a good scratch behind her collar. "No, I'm okay." Then I stepped up to the weird phone.

I picked up the handle, held it to my ear, and heard a constant tone. I at least knew to do that much. Then I tried pressing the numbers, but that didn't do anything. I checked both sides for any buttons or knobs or anything I could try.

I glanced over at Mrs. Friedrich, who thankfully turned around to grab something out of her cabinet.

Then I noticed Susanna had her eyebrows raised. She had to know something was up. "Oh, mom, I don't think her parents are home. Do you mind if I wait with Charlotte outside until we can try again later?"

"As long as you are back in time for piano lessons, dear," she said. "And Charlotte, if you need anything, you let me know, all right?"

"Yes, ma'am," I said. Then Susanna led me out of the house. Before I could make it off the front porch, I felt something grab me by the top strap of my bag and I almost fell backwards.

Susanna was holding me there. "Okay, out with it, Charlotte…if that is your real name."

"What are you talking about?" I asked, getting nervous.

Susanna let go, then folded her arms. "You're from the future, aren't you?"

Sixteen

I MUST HAVE LOOKED LIKE A DEER CAUGHT IN CAR headlights. I stood frozen on Susanna's porch. "H-h-how did you know?"

"It's kind of obvious," Susanna said. "Your clothes and the fact that you had no idea how to use a rotary phone." She glanced back over her shoulder. "I had to get you out of there before my mom noticed something was weird too. We should talk somewhere else."

I nodded and followed her back toward the neighborhood playground. We sat on the same swing set near where the lending library would be built later in the future.

"I...I don't know how much I can tell you," I said, sitting still on my swing as I already felt pretty sick to my stomach. "I don't know the rules of time travel, or even how to get back home."

"Well, I'm pretty well versed in time travel," Susanna said, pumping her legs back and forth.

"I mean, at least what I've read in books. But just to make sure you aren't trying to play a prank on me, tell me something about when you're from."

I tried to think about what would be good to say. "Uh…we have phones we carry with us in our pockets that are more powerful than the computers that were used when we first landed on the moon–"

Susanna drug her feet into the ground. "We make it to the moon?"

"Oh, oops," I said. "I guess that was in 1969…so you only have to keep that secret for a little bit? Sorry."

"Tell me more about the phones," Susanna said.

"Well, people don't use them to call each other that much. It's like a flat screen and you can see the person on the other end if you want to."

"Wow…" Susanna said. "Do you have one you can show me?"

"Sorry, my dad won't let me have one yet."

Susanna went back to pumping her legs to swing again. "So why did you come back to this time?"

"I didn't pick it. I found some of your notes in the gnome houses here and put them in a mailbox without a house behind it and someone…who I'm guessing is your dad, told me to meet him and he'd show me how it all worked and why the house was invisible. I even did a science experiment he suggested."

"Oh," Susanna said quietly.

"What?"

"It just makes sense," Susanna said, head hanging low as she scuffed the dirt with one of her tennis shoes. "My dad always thought whatever interest I took in stories wasn't worth the time, so I guess he traveled around and found someone who would be more interested in his science experiments than I was."

"But–"

"And on top of that, he had you going out and stealing my stuff from the forest so nobody would ever find it," she said. "I bet he even paid you for it."

I began to open my mouth but couldn't think of what I should say.

"Knew it," Susanna said under her breath. "Do you want to know why I spend so much time in the woods?"

"Because there are fun gnome houses to find?"

Susanna's eyes grew wet. Above, the sky had begun to darken, threatening to rain on us. "It's the only place I can still be a kid," she said. "As soon as I step in the door back home, it's homework, extra quizzes, piano lessons, violin lessons...I get one hour a day of 'unstructured time' as long as I haven't been grounded for making a B on a test, so I have to tell myself little stories to clear my head and hope that it won't be like this forever."

"How long did it take you to make your tree stump hideout?"

Susanna's eyes shot wide open. "You went in?"

I held up my hands. "It's been like half of a century...I don't think anyone else had gone in before me." I pulled my backpack off and grabbed the folder full of pictures. I began to offer it to her, then stopped.

"Wait," I said, "what happens if you see this but then you decide not to do it because you saw it?"

Susanna made a thin line out of her lips, deep in thought. "Maybe I shouldn't see whatever that is."

"I'm sorry, I just want to get home," I said. "Maybe you could deliver a message to your dad after he's figured out time travel to come back and get me, and I can just go back home and you can pretend none of this ever happened. I think he figured out time travel some time in 1983, so...in 15 years?"

"Fine," Susanna said. "I'll do it. I'll deliver your message to my dad in the future after he figures everything out and he'll know to come back and get you." She glanced down the path from the swings over to the woods. "Do you have some paper and a pen?"

I tore out a sheet of paper from my notebook and handed her my favorite pink pen. She took them and wrote a note.

"There," she said, handing the paper to me.

Dear Father,

Today, on Saturday, July 13, 1968, at 10:47 in the morning, please use your time machine to come back and take care of one of the girls you abandoned because of science.

I am referring to Charlotte Jones.

She and I are at the playground next to the forest and she wants to go home.

Sincerely,
Susanna

I checked my watch. 10:46 a.m. Assuming Susanna would be able to deliver the letter in the future and Dr. Friedrich *wanted* to come back for me, he should be coming out of the woods in exactly one minute.

We waited, both of us staring at the trail for the old man to come around the corner. It felt like the slowest minute I had ever lived through.

Then the minute passed.

No Dr. Friedrich.

"Well, that's really sad," Susanna said.

"Yeah…" I said, trying not to cry. "I guess he didn't want to come back for me."

"No," Susanna said. "My dad is a lot of things, but he isn't the type of guy who would leave a kid stuck in time. I think this means I didn't give it to him."

103

"Do you not want to?" I asked.

She shook her head. "No, I do," she said. "I think it might mean I don't make it to 1983."

"No," I said. "I think it just means he never got a letter from you."

"What?"

I took the letter in both hands, then ripped it into two and then ripped it up again until it was time travel confetti.

"We'll just have to find another way."

Susanna sniffed, then used her wrist to wipe at her nose. "Thanks," she said. "I didn't want to die young."

Then something hit me. "Hey," I said, "I think I know how to deliver a message to the future."

"How?"

"The same way you delivered messages that I found."

"A gnome house?"

I nodded. "And I know where one is just sitting around right now." I smiled, remembering the map of gnome houses we had discovered and how one of them was far away from the rest, up by our house.

I was going to send a message to my dad.

SEVENTEEN

FINDING THE ABANDONED GNOME HOUSE DR.
Friedrich had dropped wasn't tough.

Picking it up was another matter.

Susanna and I did our best to ease it to an upright
position. Once it was standing, I opened the front
door and had Susanna take a look inside.

She reached in and pulled out what remained of
the glass figures. "That's a shame."

"I'm sorry they broke," I said, kneeling down
to see the damage from when Dr. Friedrich had
dropped the mushroom house.

Susanna shook her head. "It's not that," she said,
cradling the broken fairies in her hand, careful not
to let them cut her. "I have a lot of these figures
back at home."

"Then what is it?"

"These are from my dad…a future version of him,"
she said. "I had always wondered who kept leaving

these for people to find out here in the woods, and it never crossed my mind that it would have been my dad."

"I mean…time travel isn't really something I would make my first guess," I said, closing the door on the little house.

"Oh, he hates time travel," Susanna said. "At least, the stuff they write in books. He threw away my copy of *The Time Machine* so I named our cat Weena to get back at him, but I'm not sure he'll ever know that because he won't read it."

"Maybe he did, and this is why he figured out how to go back in time and do this?" I offered.

"Well, if this is how he thinks he can make things up to me," Susanna said as she stood, "then it's too little, too late. He should have showed up and been my dad now instead of trying to sneak in a back door."

I thought about how Dr. Friedrich must have felt so much regret that he would devote the later part of his life trying to reach out to his daughter in her one hour of free time a day.

At least he was trying, but I didn't want to bring that up when Susanna seemed so angry. Besides, if I made her mad too, then I doubted I would be able to carry this really heavy house up the hill to get it to a place where my dad could find it.

"I'm sorry," I said.

"It's not your fault," Susanna replied. "Let's just get this over with."

With our limited strength, we both grabbed the lip of the mushroom house and hefted it up. As I struggled to hold up my end of the house, I figured the reason it needed to be so heavy was because it was supposed to stand the test of time.

I could sweat a little bit if it meant making it back home.

We hauled it out of the forest and to the sidewalk by the bottom of the hill. It was time to take a break, and I really wished I had a glass of water. Lightning flashed in the distance and thunder rumbled a few seconds afterward, which meant the rain was less than a mile away. I really wanted to be finished with this before that storm rolled in and made us both miserable.

With a deep breath, I leaned over and picked up my side of the house. "You ready?"

Susanna checked her watch. "We need to hurry."

"Because of the storm?"

"No, because my hour is up." she said. "My parents are going to wonder where I am. I'll be grounded for this."

"Maybe after we get this up the hill, I can tell them that you helped me and that you should get a reward?"

Susanna laughed as she struggled to help me carry the house along the sidewalk. "I'd like to see that work."

Suddenly, the sound of tires screeching came down the road and grew louder. An old, brown car pulled around the traffic circle way too fast, losing one of its hubcaps.

"I'm sorry," Susanna said, lowering the gnome house to the ground.

Inside the car I could see the younger version of Dr. Friedrich. He was furious as he pulled the car up onto the sidewalk in front of us, blocking the path up the hill.

I knew there was no easy-to-explain reason for what we were trying to do and I didn't want Susanna to get into any more trouble than she was already in.

"Oh, no," she said.

Dr. Friedrich turned off the car engine and got out, slamming the door. His face was red and a vein was bulging from his neck.

"Susanna!" he shouted. "What is going on? Your piano teacher is waiting and I am not wasting money on lessons you're not taking. This is coming out of your allowance."

"I'm sorry, Daddy," Susanna said, her head hanging low.

"And what's this?" He pointed to the gnome house. "Another one of your useless fantasies?"

He kept shouting, ignoring me. I was afraid of when that would stop being the case but I had to say something.

I thought about my family motto. *Be kind, help others…and be a friend to the lonely.* I understood lonely, and Susanna was a kindred spirit in that way.

"It's my fault," I said, stepping forward. "I was trying to get this up the hill and your daughter was helping me to–"

"I'm not talking to you, and it would better serve you to remove yourself from this conversation," he said. "I'll have a word with your parents later."

Be kind, I reminded myself. I closed my eyes and did my best to remember his old science journal. "I'm sorry, I'm not trying to make anyone even more late for piano lessons, but there's a science experiment I've been trying to understand–"

"With a giant mushroom?"

"Inside the mushroom are glass sculptures that I'm using to learn more about light refraction, and with it looking like it's about to rain–"

"You're wanting to test the prism–"

"I'm wanting to test a theory about how light could be captured at different speeds," I said, hoping I was remembering everything right. "The mushroom is a diorama…a really heavy one that Susanna was helping me carry."

"What are you trying to prove?" Dr. Friedrich asked, crossing his arms.

I shrugged. "That maybe there could be a balance between learning and…fun."

Dr. Friedrich stared at me for what felt like forever, then gave a little sniff. He turned his eyes back toward his daughter. "Maybe your time spent with this one isn't entirely wasted if this is how you are choosing to use your unstructured hour. But the fact remains that your piano teacher is waiting. Get in the car, now."

Susanna whispered, "I'm sorry."

"Me too," I said.

She walked to the brown car and her dad gave me an odd look as they both got in. Then they took off, leaving me with an incredibly heavy gnome house and no way to get it up the hill.

I tried picking it up, but could only get a step before I tripped over myself. This thing was heavier than Petals.

Thinking of Petals made me want to cry. How would Mom and Dad explain to her that I was gone? Would I wind up an old lady by the time I would get to see them again?

I couldn't let that happen.

Tipping the mushroom house on its side, I began trying to roll it up the hill. It took a lot of effort and a couple of times it rolled back on me until I stopped to find a big enough rock by the side of the street to prop underneath it when I got tired.

I had made it halfway up the hill and my arms and legs felt like they were made of jelly that was on fire. I would never skip one of my gym classes ever again if I made it back.

Then I heard the sound of a propeller engine getting louder.

I saw a young Mr. Adams launching his flying machine down the hill. It was getting closer and closer. He was looking up at the skies and not at me!

I let go of the mushroom house and dove out of the way just as he saw me. At the last second, he swerved and his flying machine ran off the street and hit the sidewalk curb, throwing him out of the machine and wrecking it.

Eighteen

I RUSHED OVER TO THE WRECKAGE, HEARING PLENTY of words coming from Mr. Adams that I knew I would be in really big trouble if I ever repeated.

"I'm so, so sorry!" I shouted. "Are you all right?"

Mr. Adams was busy trying to get himself out of the loose parachute that had wrapped him up inside of it. I could see on the side where he had painted *Betsy II* in swooping white letters next to the bent up frame.

Now I knew how he had gotten from *Betsy II* to *Betsy III*.

Mr. Adams, who was maybe in his mid-20s, freed himself from the parachute and gave me a long look. "Where did you come from?"

I pointed back to the neighborhood at the foot of the hill. "I'm sorry, I didn't know you were taking off."

"Nobody comes up this hill except the mailman and me," Mr. Adams said. "Wasn't expecting you."

He stepped over to the bent up cage and checked out *Betsy II*. "This is going to take forever to fix." He took off his goggles and ran his hand through his shaggy brown hair. "What are you even doing up here?"

"Uh...I was wanting to put a time capsule on top of the hill...for a project."

"It's the summer," Mr. Adams said, pulling off his flight gloves. "School is out."

"It's not for school," I said. "It's a...family thing." The mushroom house had rolled over to the curb and thankfully not all the way down to the bottom of the hill.

"Why not just put it in your backyard?" he asked.

That was kind of the point, but I couldn't tell him my backyard wasn't a backyard yet. "Um...I haven't gotten approval from the..." I tried to think about what it was Mr. Adams had said when I first met him. "Home...owning..."

"Homeowners association," Mr. Adams said, narrowing his eyes. "I know all about them. If you're waiting on the HOA, you'll be waiting for a long time," he said. "Took me three years to get old *Betsy* cleared for takeoff, and that was with some greased wheels."

Not really knowing what greasy wheels had to do with anything, I nodded like I understood. "Yes, exactly," I said. "And I have no grease, so that's why I thought I would put it up here on some land that wasn't built on yet."

Mr. Adams took a deep breath. "Well, if you help me push *Betsy* back up the hill we'll load your... mushroom time capsule...thing onto her."

That was a deal I was very willing to make. He picked up the mushroom house and placed it on the bent frame of *Betsy*, and together we rolled both projects up the hill. He did most of the work, but I helped as much as my tired muscles would let me.

The downpour began as soon as we made it to his driveway.

"Probably wasn't the smartest idea to go flying when a storm was so close," Mr. Adams said. "You might have saved my life."

He let me hide inside his little garage so I wouldn't get soaked and I saw only a couple of the neighborhood photographs hanging on the wall. He would have many more flights ahead of him.

Lowering the gnome house to the garage floor, Mr. Adams said, "Why did you make this so heavy? Don't tell me you're going to try and bury it."

I shook my head as I took off my backpack, hoping my notebook hadn't gotten wet. Thankfully it had stayed dry, so I pulled out my pen and began to write a note to my dad.

"What's today's date again?" I asked.

Mr. Adams looked at me, confused, then, "Saturday, July 13, 1968. You sure I didn't run into you or something?"

I nodded, going back to writing my note. Then I stopped. If I asked Dr. Friedrich to come back today and he didn't, then all hope was lost. There might have been some reason he couldn't come back twice in the same day. And also, I felt bad for leaving Susanna in trouble, so I decided to ask for him to come back on July 14th instead of today. I could make it one night if I needed to. I had been in Girl Scouts, after all.

> *Dear Dad,*
>
> *I am so sorry I didn't trust you. I know reading this is going to be so weird and I promise I'm not making any of this up. I'm writing you from the past because the invisible house was actually a time machine.*
>
> *Dr. Friedrich doesn't know he stranded me in time, so what I need you to do is find him by leaving a letter in his mailbox. I don't think mailing it works. You have to put something in the box without Otto seeing you. Then you tell him that I am stuck in July 14, 1968 and if he can come back and get me, then I should hopefully be home and it won't have been much time for you that I have been gone.*
>
> *Again, I am so, so sorry and all I want is to be with you and Mom and Petals again and have a really big family hug and play home movies and never get separated from you all again.*

I love you all so much and I really hope I
see you again soon.

Love,
Charlotte

I finished my letter, then folded it up tight. I saw that the little door on the mushroom base had a rubber seal around it, so I figured it would be safe just like Susanna's notes had been.

By now, the rain had really started to pour down, and I took a deep breath and began rolling the mushroom house out to the lot across from Mr. Adams's place.

It was still mostly trees where my house was going to be built, so it took a lot of effort to find a path that would go back far enough that it wouldn't eventually get destroyed. I wished I had remembered more about my new house and how deep the backyard was.

I tried to imagine playing home movies with my family and thought about how much we ran around chasing Petals. I figured the farther back the better, so it took me almost an hour to get the house into a place that I could be a little extra sure Dad would be able to find it someday.

Then it hit me. Someone needed to tell my dad that it was there in case he never found it himself.

Drenched, I ran back over to Mr. Adams's house just in time to see his pickup truck drive down the hill with the wreckage of *Betsy II* in the back. I really wished I had thought to ask him to relay the message beforehand.

I started walking carefully down the hill so I wouldn't slip on the slick road and fall on my backside and slide the rest of the way down. I was starting to feel a little extra hungry and didn't know when I would get another meal.

If I was trapped here, there was a lot I was going to have to figure out.

I finally made it back to Susanna's house and saw the brown car sitting in her driveway. Dr. Friedrich was home and I was scared to talk to him again after how he had treated poor Susanna. I could hear piano music coming from inside the house.

I approached the door and put my hand up to knock.

But before I could, someone tapped me on the shoulder.

I spun around to see who it was.

Mrs. Friedrich.

Nineteen

Mrs. Friedrich and I shared a long look as I waited for her to break the silence. Then she smiled and I realized something was different about her.

First, she wasn't wearing the same outfit I had seen her in when she was in the kitchen. Second, when she smiled she seemed almost more like an older sister to Susanna than a mother.

"Figure it out yet?" she asked.

"You're…no," I said as everything came together in my mind.

This was Susanna, but maybe in her 20s or 30s. "He let you time travel?"

"'*Let me*' is maybe a little too strong of a way to put it," she said, crossing her arms, "but we need to get out of here before anyone else sees us."

My mind spun as I followed this older Susanna down the sidewalk. She handed me a black umbrella and I was relieved not to have the rain pour down on me so hard. "I have so many questions."

"As you should," Susanna said, walking faster than I could easily keep pace with. "And I can only answer so many of them or else you and I will both get in trouble." She turned and smiled at me.

"How did you find me?"

"Well, this wasn't a hard date to remember, meeting a time traveler and all…" she bobbed her head from side to side. "So as soon as I passed my exams and joined the Society of Time Travelers, this was my first stop."

Society of Time Travelers? I thought. *That's a thing?*

"So that's why your dad wouldn't have shown up when we wrote the note," I said. "You were going to be the one to come back and get me?"

"Well, I may get in trouble for this and lose my license, but I couldn't leave you stuck here," she said.

Ahead, a house sat on the formerly empty lot. The mailbox was the same, though. A boxy mail truck was parked outside of it, its engine still running.

As we neared, a familiar old mailman stepped out.

"Otto?" I asked, my jaw dropping. He was the exact same age as he was in the future. Either he didn't age or he could time travel as well. "You're in on this, too?"

It suddenly all started to make sense. The only times I had seen him were when I had delivered something to Dr. Friedrich's mailbox or when he was delivering something to me from Dr. Friedrich. I never even thought to check who delivered the mail normally.

He tipped his blue cap to me. "Ah, Miss Carefree Valley Charlotte." He put his hand over his heart. "Neither snow, nor rain, nor heat, nor gloom of night, nor time wormholes, nor...well, I guess I can't complete that without sharing too much, now, can I?"

Susanna gave a wide smile. "You have to keep Otto's secret," she said. "He could get in big trouble for making the unauthorized deliveries between you and my dad."

"Oh, she was going to know soon enough," he said. "I mean, she *is* Charlotte Jones after all."

I looked at Susanna, confused. "What does that mean?"

Susanna smacked Otto's arm. "I think maybe our favorite time traveling mailman should get back to work and not spoil anything else."

"Yes, ma'am," he said, nodding to me and tipping his blue cap to Susanna. "Many deliveries to make, but at least I've got time on my side, right?"

I had a feeling he liked to say that a lot. He drove off down the street and disappeared as he turned a corner.

"So the mailbox is here to deliver mail through time?" I asked.

"That's one use for it," Susanna said, walking me up to the house. "It's also a beacon for houses to find their way in time. My father's technology acts as kind of a...how do I put it...time travel vacation club? You would think there would be cars or phone booths or police call boxes to get you back and forth through time and space, but having a system like this where there are only so many lots where and when you can travel makes things a bit easier to deal with. It's hard to lose a house in the system."

We entered the house and while the place looked almost exactly the same on the outside, inside it was completely different.

"This isn't your father's house..." I said, noticing that the floor plan was changed. The inside was light blue and decorated with paint by numbers of pretty farms and sleepy sea towns. "Why is it different inside?"

Susanna shook her head. "What you snuck into was my dad's retirement house. No matter what the house actually looks like, when it arrives here it appears the same so it doesn't seem out of place. For this neighborhood, it will always look like the house I grew up in. This one is mine."

"What is it exactly that you do?" I asked.

Susanna sucked at her teeth in thought. "Well, I can't tell you until you sign the paperwork promising you'll keep all of this a secret."

I really didn't like the idea of not being able to tell Mom and Dad anything. "And what if I don't?"

Susanna gave me a long look. "Hey, you did me a really big favor when you talked to my dad today. It may have not seemed like much, but after a while it got to him. But by the time he really had a change of heart, I was about ready to move out of the house and he started the whole mission to figure out time travel so he could try to be a better dad during the one hour a day I had free."

"How did that work?" I asked.

"After a while, instead of leaving gnome houses for me to find, he actually came and talked to me," Susanna said. "Things got a lot better after that. So I'm trying to keep you and your family out of big trouble with the time authorities. Would you rather be stuck?"

I shook my head. "But my dad would have seen me disappear," I said. "He's going to know something is weird."

"Not if we return you to the exact same spot when you traveled back in time," Susanna said, looking out the window.

"Then how would that explain that the house had appeared when it was gone before?" I asked. "He saw it."

Susanna tapped a finger on her chin. "You've got a good point."

"So he can sign the paperwork too?" I asked.

"I suppose he'll have to," Susanna said. "It's either that or a memory wipe."

My eyes went wide.

"I'm kidding...kind of." Susanna opened a desk drawer and pulled out a badge. She handed it to me. "Usually we don't let people who are so young into our ranks, but you're going to be an exception. Besides, your paperwork is already filed at the Time Bureau, so who cares if you get this badge a little bit early. It's hard enough to keep track of when people sign stuff anyway."

She pressed a button on the desk and the machine down in the basement began to groan to life beneath us. "Now, here's my favorite part."

Outside, the sun and moon started to spin around faster and faster until they became streaks again.

"I love watching this because it reminds me that life passes in front of us with so many stories, and I wish I could see them all, but we get just as much time as everyone else. So while we have more opportunities to go places, we still have to choose very carefully what we should be doing with our time."

"So you're saying we still have to make every day count?" I asked.

"That's right." She walked over to the front door, then checked her watch. "Now, we're right back in the moment you would have disappeared," she said. "Well, like half a second later so my house and my dad's house don't crash into each other."

The doorbell chimed.

Susanna gave me a confused look, then turned the knob and opened the door. "Oh, hi, Dad."

Twenty

A HOLOGRAM OF THE OLDER DR. FRIEDRICH STOOD on the front porch. I could see through him into the front yard and thought this must have been like a really fancy video call. "Now, is everything set right?"

"Yes, I think so," Susanna said. "Charlotte, I'd like you to officially meet my dad."

I hadn't gotten a good look at the older version of him yet. He had a big, bushy gray mustache, and what little wisps of hair were left on the top of his head danced back and forth when he moved. The harshness in his eyes from when I last saw him was gone, thankfully.

"It's nice to meet you," I said. "I'm sorry I was disrespectful back in the past."

He waved a hand at me. "Oh, pish posh," he said. "I was holding the reins a little too tight on sweet Susanna and you helped me see that. Once I learned that she loved gnomes and rainbows and all of the fanciful stuff I never let her play with, I devoted my retirement to creating things that I hoped could still give her a sense of the wonder and mystery that I tried too hard to keep her from. And wouldn't you know it, that led me straight to you. It's funny how time works out, isn't it?" He faced his daughter. "Does she know yet?"

Susanna shook her head.

"Know what?" I asked.

"All good things come in due time," Dr. Friedrich said with a smile that made his bushy gray mustache spread wide.

"Oh, I forgot to say thank you for the fountain pen," I said. "It was a really nice birthday gift."

"I was honored to give you your first one," Dr. Friedrich said. "And if you ever need penmanship lessons...well, my handwriting needs a lot of work, so perhaps Susanna can help you there."

"Are we going to see each other again?" I asked.

"We're...not allowed to say," Susanna said, hiding a grin. "But I think the odds are pretty good."

"Just drop us a letter," Dr. Friedrich said. "Oh, and be sure to use the correct postage this time so Otto doesn't get into any hot water."

Susanna smiled, then reached into a small purse and handed me a book of shimmery stamps. They looked like just blank blue squares, but slowly faded into the flag stamp I was used to seeing.

"What are these?" I asked.

"Forever and ever stamps," Dr. Friedrich said. "They change to appear like they belong in whatever time period they are in. Keeps our mail delivery folks safe."

"Thank you," I said, holding up the stamps. I really wanted to get back and see my family again, so I stepped through the door. "I promise I'll write."

Susanna and hologram Dr. Friedrich waved at me. As soon as I made it past the mailbox, I heard the whirring sound from the house.

In front of me, time unfroze. The door to Oliver slammed shut and Dad stepped out onto the sidewalk.

I rushed over and threw my arms around him, almost crying because I was so happy.

"Hey, kiddo, are you okay?" Dad asked.

I just hugged him tighter.

"What...why are you soaking wet?"

I had forgotten I was still drenched from the rain earlier. I let go of the hug and smiled. "It's a long story."

"Does it explain why a house showed up and then went away?"

I turned around to see the empty lot. "It does."

Dad pulled his phone out and opened up the picture he had taken of Dr. Friedrich's house. "Because I'm not crazy, it *was* there."

"It was," I said. "I want to show you something back at our place."

As Dad drove Oliver back up our hill, I did my best to tell him everything about what had happened in 1968 with the Friedrich family and how we're supposed to keep it all a secret.

I confessed to breaking his fountain pen and apologized and explained that Dr. Friedrich had gotten it fixed. There were parts of the story about time travel I didn't understand entirely, and by the time we reached our driveway, Dad sat there, stunned.

"Remember the map we saw and there was one gnome house over by us?" I asked, handing him the folder of printed out photos.

"Sure do," Dad said.

"Well, I put it there in 1968."

We got out and walked around to the back-yard, where Mom was sitting on the back patio and Petals was hopping around on one foot pretending to be another one of her favorite animals.

"How did it go?" Mom called out.

"Our daughter is a time traveler," Dad said.

"That's nice," Mom said. "Petals is a one-legged kangaroo because the other foot touched lava."

"Lava!" Petals shouted.

I would explain to Mom and my one-legged kangaroo sister what had happened later, but for now, I was on the hunt for the mushroom house.

We passed by the tree with the tire swing and about twenty feet into the woods I found what I was looking for.

It had kind of sunk into the dirt on one side so it was leaning to the left. I turned and smiled at Dad. "See?"

Double-checking the printed out photo, Dad scratched his head. "How is any of this possible?"

"Maybe I can get Dr. Friedrich to explain it," I said as I kneeled down and opened the little door at the base of the mushroom.

My note was gone.

Instead, a nice, fresh looking envelope sat inside with a small box.

"Did you find it?" Dad asked.

I pulled out the letter and package, showing it to him. The front of it was addressed to me, written on a typewriter. The return label said *S. Friedrich, SoTT.*

"Another note from Susanna?" Dad asked. "Go on, what does it say?"

Carefully, I opened the back of the envelope. I knew I would want to keep this forever. As I unfolded the papers, there was a letter on top and a few official looking forms behind it.

Dear Charlotte,

On behalf of the Society of Time Travelers, I want to welcome you and your family into our membership.

The secret of our existence must be kept, and I am including several blank forms for the rest of your family to complete and mail in. Don't worry about having your brother fill one out yet.

Just leave the forms in my father's mailbox and Otto will know what to do. The package has the SoTT badges for the rest of your family like the one I gave you.

I wish to thank you once more for your bravery and kindness. You have a bright future ahead of you, and anytime you wish to go on another adventure in the past, or explore the future, just let me know.

Welcome to the Society of Time Travelers. There are mysteries yet to be solved, and we will need your help.

> *Yours past, present, and future,*
> *Susanna Friedrich*
> *Senior Director of the*
> *Society of Time Travelers*

I showed Dad the letter and his eyes went wide. "And all that because you found a mailbox without a house behind it?"

I opened the box of badges and handed the one with Dad's name on it to him. He held it up to the light to inspect it, then flipped it over. "Huh," he said. "Does yours say the same thing?"

"What do you mean?" I pulled out my Society of Time Travelers badge and looked at the back of it.

It read:

> *Be kind,*
> *help others,*
> *and make every*
> *day count.*
>
> *–Charlotte Jones*
> *Society of Time Travelers*

About the Author

C.W. Task was born in a pandemic during a long father/daughter neighborhood walk when schools were let out and work was remote in more ways than one.

The Invisible House is C.W.'s first book, but due to the joy created over finding quality time and creativity in otherwise difficult circumstances, it will not be their last.

Made in the USA
Monee, IL
22 September 2020

42449738R00090